Library of Congress Cataloging-in-Publication Data

Albert, Bill
Desert blues / by Bill Albert
p. cm.
Summary: When a car accident makes sixteen-year-old Harold an orphan and sends him to live with his Aunt Enid in the Californian desert, he and she both find they have to make adjustments to their lives.
ISBN 1-877946-49-4 (cloth) : $22.00
[1. Aunts--Fiction. 2. Orphans--Fiction. 3. California--Fiction.] I. Title
PZ7 .A3175De 1994
[Fic]--dc20 93-36289
CIP
AC

Manufactured in the United States of America

First Edition, December 1994 --1600 copies

THE PERMANENT PRESS
Noyac Road
Sag Harbor, NY 11963

Harold and Enid

Freeway Driving

Harold always knew that his father was a stinking, lousy driver but just how stinking and how lousy he didn't find out until the day the old man tried to make a U-turn on the Pasadena Freeway.

They were on their way to Palm Springs for the weekend to visit his aunt, his mother's younger sister. When his mother said they were going his father had protested. He always did. It never made any difference.

"But we never go this time of year. July is murder there. You can fry eggs on the sidewalk. Maybe we should wait until October or something. Wadda you say, Sylvia?"

"What do I say? I say no. You're not going to melt, Norman, or fry on the sidewalk like an egg, and besides, I want to see my sister. For Christ sake, it's only two days!"

"Jesus, Sylvia, you know she hates me! And two days is two days. You and the boy go. OK? I'll be fine here by myself."

"Norman, *she* doesn't hate you, it's *you*! *You* hate *her*! And the boy's name is Harold."

"For the love of God! Sylvia, please!"

"No pleases. No! And, if you don't go how are we supposed to get there? The Greyhound? Five hours with a lot of cowboys and *shvartzers*, stopping in every cockamamy town from Azusa to Banning? Is that what you expect me to do? Is it?"

"You should learn to drive," he said lamely, the battle slipping from his grasp, the war long since lost.

His mother snorted dismissively and strode out of the room.

"Sylvia! I don't... Ah, hell!"

His father slumped down in his easy chair, staring vacantly at the wall through heavy horn-rimmed glasses. His hands knotted into small fists. He held the fists up in front of him as if trying to decide what to do with them. Harold knew there was nothing his father could do with them. He never had. He never would.

Harold was sitting in the far corner of the room trying not to be noticed. However, the corner wasn't far enough away for not being noticed.

"Wadda you think, Harry? You wanna go down there?"

He didn't have to ask. Harold hated the long tedious drive, his parents' constant quarreling, his father's nervy erratic driving. And at the end of it there was Aunt Enid. Every time she saw him she gushed all over him, pinching and cooing as if he were still a small baby.

"So big, Harold! How did you get so big? Give your Aunt Enid a nice kiss. Come on, darling, I haven't seen you forever!"

She stank of flowery perfume. When she got near him the sickly-sweet vapors pushed uninvited up Harold's nose. Aunt Enid's odor clung to his clothes for days.

And Palm Springs. At home, in Los Angeles, he had his records, his friends, seven different TV stations, and the endless selection of dark, forbidden movie theaters on Hollywood Boulevard. In Palm Springs he didn't know any kids, there were only three movie theaters, if you didn't include the Sun-Air Drive-In, which the carless Harold didn't, and only four TV stations. In short, there was nothing to do. Nothing, that is, for an overweight redheaded kid who sweated a lot and whose skin burned a stinging pink in the desert sun. No, Palm Springs was a place for golfers and tennis players and guys that pretended to be cowboys; in other words, a place for jerks. It was most definitely not for Harold Abelstein. He saw himself as strictly a big-city sidewalks kind of guy.

"Come on, Harold darling, the pool is lovely and cool. Why don't you get into a pair of trunks?"

"Uh, no thanks, Aunt Enid."

"It's not healthy, a big boy like you staying in the house all day long. Fresh air. You need fresh air, not TV all the time. Ten, fifteen minutes, that's all. I promise you, you won't burn. Look, darling, the sun is almost behind the mountain."

He tried not to notice the curls of dark pubic hair that escaped from the crotch of her swimsuit or her breasts, large, oily-brown and strapped loosely to her chest with a bikini top.

Everything about Aunt Enid made him uncomfortable. Mascara gave her eyes a look of perpetual surprise, her mouth was too big, swollen to an unnatural size by bright red lipstick. She talked loudly and touched everyone. Not even the milkman was safe. With red-nailed fingers she would tap out secret messages on his arm while ordering a pound of butter, an extra quart of milk. Harold didn't like being touched.

The only thing that kept him sane on those long weekends was the certain knowledge that they were only long weekends. That soon he would be home again, away from the sun, the heat, the endless desert sand, and especially away from his aunt's unavoidable, overripe body.

* * *

He rarely listened to his parents' constant arguments. Their quarrels were the background static of his life. Only when he heard his own name would he tune in, and then very cautiously, not wanting to hear too much. So, he could never remember exactly what they were arguing about before his father missed the turnoff for the San Bernadino Freeway. What happened immediately afterwards he could never forget.

"Norman, now look what you've done! Why don't you pay attention?"

"Huh?"

"The freeway, the freeway! You're on the wrong one! Pasadena! Pasadena! We're on our way to Pasadena. You know somebody there maybe? Somebody maybe you're not telling me about?"

"What? Who? Hey, I couldn't..."

"Look, for God sake!"

At this point Harold began to listen more closely. He looked out the window to see if they actually had taken the wrong freeway. The pale blur of stucco tract houses on both sides of the road told him nothing.

It was very hot in the car. Harold was sweating and could hardly breathe. His father said if you kept the windows closed the smog wouldn't get in. He'd heard there was a lot of smog in Pasadena.

Soon they were in the far right hand lane and moving slowly.

Now Harold could make out the individual houses with their thin green lawns and new wooden fences. The driver behind them honked. Immediately another, louder deeper horn sounded, followed by the hiss of air brakes and the squeal of tires. Harold did not turn around.

"If you hadn't been *yenting* on and on at me, Sylvia..."

"A *yente*, am I? A *yente*! Sure, sure, always my fault, isn't it? God, I don't know about you, Norman, I really don't."

"You don't know *what* about me?" his father shouted, his hands tightening on the wheel, his voice rising in an indignant squeak.

They were now in the emergency lane, moving about five miles an hour. A steady stream of traffic rushed by them. The wind displaced by the big trucks rocked them gently from side to side. Finally, his father stopped the car. His mother's voice rose another quarrelsome octave.

"So, now we have to go all the way to Pasadena I suppose? An extra hour, maybe more. Dumb, Norman. Really, really dumb. We'll have to stop so I can call Enid. You know she's expecting us for lunch? Norman? Norman, what do you think you're doing? Norman!"

He had put the car in reverse, rolled down the window, stuck his head out and was backing up, apparently searching for the misplaced San Bernadino Freeway. His wife continued to shout, to pull at his shirt, but Harold's father was through listening.

After a few minutes he stopped. He pulled his head back into the car, straightened his glasses. His thin face was contorted. Harold saw flecks of saliva bubbling at the corners of his mouth. He thought it was the effects of the Pasadena smog pouring in through the carelessly opened window. Almost immediately he realized it wasn't the smog.

"You don't wanna go to Pasadena?" his father screamed. "Right, no Pasadena! No *fucking* Pasadena for the Abelsteins!'

"NORMAN!!'

Harold threw himself from the back seat to the floor of the car.

* * *

Harold had come to lying in a hospital bed. He tried to move but had to close his eyes against the pain which bayoneted through his forehead. He lay very still. When he opened his eyes again, a young man in a white coat was standing next to the bed looking down at him. He picked up Harold's wrist, checked his watch.

"How do you feel now, Harold?"

His head ached, and he was sick to his stomach.

"Huh? Oh, fine, I guess."

The man patted his arm.

"Good. Very good. I'm glad to see you're back with us."

Back, Harold thought. Where have I been? Then he remembered.

The freeway. His mother shouting then screaming, a drawn out howl weaving its way through the sound of tearing metal and breaking glass as the car was flung over on its side. He had tried to hold onto the floor, to dig his fingernails into the thin carpet. It was impossible. He let go. Something hit him on the side of the head.

He was lying on the road. He could feel pieces of gravel digging into his back. Otherwise there was no pain. There was little sensation at all. Flashing red lights, men shouting, sirens. The picture faded. He was staring up at the man in the white coat.

"Where's my mom? Dad?" he asked, panic blurring his voice.

The man didn't answer. He studied Harold's medical notes. After a couple of minutes he hooked the metal clipboard to the end of the bed and smiled at Harold.

"You just rest now, son. Dr. Mason will be in to see you in a little while."

"Where's my mom?" Harold shouted, as the door swung closed behind the man in the white coat.

Almost immediately the door was swung back the other way and a nurse came into the room. She was very short, her muscular legs encased in thick white stockings. She marched over to Harold's bed.

"Now, now what's all this shouting, Harold? We don't allow shouting in here. This is a hospital, you know, not a playground."

"But where..." Harold began to say.

He didn't get any further. A cold thermometer was thrust under his tongue.

"Um, ah, mu,"he spluttered.

"Under your tongue, young man. Close your mouth. No talking."

Bristles of black hair poked up from the side of a large reddish wart on the nurse's upper lip. She was so close to him that he couldn't not stare at it. He looked up from the wart and straight into the nurse's flinty-dark eyes. They glared at him over the top of the wart. He was too startled to look away. He was caught in the glare of her eyes like a jackrabbit on a nighttime highway.

After a couple of minutes she yanked the thermometer from under his tongue.

"Fine," she said. "Good."

"My mother. Where's my mother? My father?"

The nurse looked away. She straightened the sheets, took the clipboard and wrote something down.

"Nurse?"

A cold knot took hold in his stomach. He knew something terrible had happened. The chill spread into his chest.

"Doctor will explain everything to you. You've had a nasty bump on the head. Just rest now."

Why did everyone tell him to rest?

They nurse left the room. He was alone again.

They were dead. They had to be dead. Or at least very badly hurt. Why else would nobody tell him anything?

It was his fault. He had willed it. In fact, his daydream fantasy alternated between everyone feeling sorry for him because he was an orphan and his parents standing over his grave, guilty for all the times they had yelled at him, punished him. All their injustices repaid with his death. But, he was alive, they were dead.

Half an hour later an older man in a white coat came into the room.

"Hello, Harold," he said, sitting on the edge of the bed. "I'm Dr. Mason."

Dr. Mason's cheeks were deeply creased, his eyes sad. Years of giving people bad news. Harold knew his bad news was on its way.

"How do you feel, Harold?"

"OK, thanks."

He didn't want to ask the doctor about his parents. Maybe if he didn't ask they would be alright. He wanted them to be alright.

After all, he did love them. At least he supposed he did. They were his parents. He knew that deep down, below the day-to-day stuff, everyone loved their parents. Only, sometimes he had wondered whether they really were his parents.

"You got red hair in your family, Sylvia?"

"A hundred times, Norman, a hundred times the same question. I got the same answer. No. No red hair. Satisfied?"

"Yeah, but listen, I suppose it happens sometimes?"

"Sure," she said, "it happens, sometimes it happens."

Both his parents had dark brown hair and brown eyes. A red-haired green-eyed son led to lots of jokes about the iceman. Harold had never seen an iceman.

The doctor took a pencil flashlight from his pocket.

"Now look straight ahead please."

The light shined deep into Harold's eye.

"Right, now the other one. Uh-huh. Thank you. Well, Harold, I think you're going to be 100%. A little concussion and some cuts and bruises. You're a very lucky boy. You remember what happened?"

"Uh, sort of. Not much of it though."

"You know it was a serious accident, don't you?"

"Yeah, I suppose."

"Well, I'm afraid it was much worse for your mother and father, Harold."

Harold looked down at his hands. They were soft fat hands. Red freckled hands. He didn't like his hands very much. They reminded him of his body, which he also didn't like. Puppy fat, his mother said. It would go in time, she said. That didn't make him feel any better about the rolls around his middle or his thick white thighs. It was definitely not the body he wanted. Not athletic, not built for dancing or surfing or getting a tan or most of the other things kids his age were doing. Of course, he knew that he didn't actually want to dance or surf or waste time getting a tan because it was all pretty dumb stuff, but he also didn't want to be too white, too fat and too slow. He closed his eyes and let his head fall back on the pillow.

The doctor cleared his throat.

"You know they're dead, don't you, son? Your parents."

Harold nodded. He didn't look at the doctor.

"I'm sorry. Really sorry. There's nothing anyone can say to you to make it right."

Harold was numb. He didn't know where to begin. He felt completely empty.

The door opened. He looked up. It was Aunt Enid. She'd been crying. Harold burst into tears.

Starting Over

He wished he had known more about his parents, but, when he got around to wishing it was too late.

His father had worked in a bank downtown, but exactly what he did there was a mystery to Harold. He never talked about his job, except to complain. His boss had been dissatisfied with something he had done, promotion had been given to someone younger. On and on. He was not a happy person. Neither was Harold's mother. She was often testy and impatient with Harold, and she fought with his father all the time. Everything, anything could trigger off an argument. Harold never understood why they married. Tender moments between them were rare. There wasn't a lot of laughter around at the Abelsteins'.

Most of his friends had similar stories to tell about life at home. That made Harold feel better. It was nothing to do with him, it was the way of the world. He made a firm promise to himself never to get married. He stayed out of the house as much as he could.

His father had no family. His parents had died when he was in his teens, there were no brothers or sisters, no cousins, aunts or uncles that Harold had ever heard of. Nobody, except his wife and son. On his mother's side there was only Aunt Enid.

"We're going to get along just fine together, aren't we, Harold darling?" Aunt Enid said.

Once in a while his mother or father had mentioned something about their childhoods or their parents, but Harold had never paid too much attention to what was said. Why Uncle Hyman's fur business had collapsed in 1929, a long-dead cousin's doomed romance with a Turk, how they had driven across the country after the war to start a new life in California. These and other infrequent, scattered pieces of family history had meant nothing to him. They were dim events with no real connection to him or to his life. Now, when he felt the need to understand his own life by reconstructing his parents, all he had were scraps of badly remembered conversations, a box of old photographs and, of course, Aunt Enid.

"Look, dear, this will be your room. A nice bed, a little desk where you can do your homework. Do you like it?"

The room was small. Not more than eight or nine feet square, with a window looking out on the front yard and the street. He reached out and touched one of the large red roses which covered the walls. They were thick-petaled, throbbing with life. He wondered how many there were in the room. He would have to count them. He would have a lot of time for counting.

"Yes, I know, dear. I know. You see, it was my dressing room."

She patted him on the arm. Harold tensed, but held his ground. He didn't want to offend his aunt. He had no place else to go.

"As soon as we can, we'll get rid of the roses. OK? Not the kind of wallpaper a big boy wants in his room. I know that. It's just everything has been rather sudden. You understand, don't you, darling?"

He didn't like it when she called him "a big boy". It made him feel like a kid and he was almost fifteen and three-quarters.

* * *

Harold sat on the bed and stared at the walls. Roses. He really hated roses. And the room smelled of Aunt Enid. In the hall the air cooler gurgled and groaned. He looked through the window. Outside it was diamond bright and very hot. He sighed deeply and put his head in his hands. He had become an exile in the desert. An exile in a stinky prison cell swarming with man-eating roses.

Until he had to face living with his strange aunt in a strange town he didn't realize how easy the expectations of his life in Los Angeles had been. Before the accident when he had thought about his life at all, it was to think how much better it would be if his parents were different, if school was different, if they had a nicer place to live instead of the cramped two-bedroom apartment on the wrong side of La Brea. But at least then he had had his own room without stupid roses, all his stuff, his friends, the record shops, the movie theaters. He missed all that. He even missed school, the neighborhood and his parents. They had always been there. He had assumed they always would be.

He looked around him. At the room, at the suitcases, at the boxes on the floor. He tried to imagine the shape of his new life. He couldn't. There was nothing to construct it out of, nothing really to expect. Nothing that is, except Aunt Enid and he didn't know what to expect from her. She seemed to spend most of her time either out with her friends or sitting by the pool half-naked. That didn't connect with anything he knew about. Exactly how, exactly where, was he going to fit in?

Aunt Enid. How was he going to live with Aunt Enid? She was so damn attentive. He couldn't make a move without her fussing over him, grabbing hold of parts of parts of his body and telling him everything would be alright. On balance he preferred his mother's nagging. He had been able to ignore that more easily. He couldn't even escape to the movies or with his friends as he had in LA. Venturing out the door into the summer desert was dangerous, and he was blocks from the center of town. To make matters worse, what he had seen of the center hadn't been very promising. Most of the stores were closed and there seemed to be no people. A ghost town.

He took his shirts out of the suitcase. They had been ironed and neatly folded. A white label with his name in faded ink was on the inside of one collar.

Y camp. His mother had packed for him. She spent days sewing labels on everything — shirts, underwear, socks, one label on each sock. H. ABELSTEIN. They rubbed his skin raw. When he waved good-bye from the window of the bus, his mother yelled at him to be careful, to write every week. Then as the bus pulled away she began to weep. She trotted a few yards alongside the bus shouting his name and more instructions. He looked away hoping the other boys would think she was someone else's mother.

He hated Y camp. Too much hearty outdoors stuff and all that forced Christian good fellowship. There was no way out even for the Jewish kids. At Blue Lake Y-Camp everyone was a Christian, every Kaplan and Klein, every Abelstein and Zuckerman. The cabins were too small and smelled of unwashed bodies and camp-food farts. The outside toilets were worse, just wooden huts built over big holes in the ground, steaming in the summer heat with the accumulated shit of innumerable campers. At least now he wouldn't have to go back to Blue Lake Y Camp.

Good-bye, good-bye our beloved Blue Lake
All winter long our hearts will ache
Until again the pine trees call
We will miss you, one and all.

He sighed and took more clothes out of the suitcase.

Each summer his father had talked about taking him fishing.

"Sure Harry, I'll get a couple of days off and we'll take the party boat out from Malibu. Get up early, have breakfast on the road. Just the two of us. Wadda you say?"

Like most of his father's plans, the fishing never happened. Something always came up to postpone the trip. But Harold hadn't minded then. He was no sailor. Even rowing in MacArthur Park made him nauseous.

He finished putting his clothes away in the closet and the chest of drawers. Then he began to look over his most precious possession — his record collection. Four large cardboard boxes of 45s, carefully arranged in alphabetical order. He could remember every record down to the color of the label. It was his claim to fame at Fairfax High and had made him popular with, or at the least tolerated by, the few Negro guys at the school. It gave him a piece of territory and that was important, especially for a shambling, vulnerable-looking fat kid who didn't run with any crowd. The hoods, the Brylcreemed, leather-jacketed hard cases, mostly left him alone.

"Hey, Red," shouted Tyrone Price, "What you got for *Let the Good Times Roll*?"

A food fight was going on in one corner of the school yard. There was a rumble of shouting, kids running back and forth. A carton of milk arched high in the air and splattered against the wall near where Harold was standing. He moved to one side. Milk dribbled down the wall and onto the ground at his feet.

"Come on, Red! Come on, man, *Let the Good Times Roll*!"

It was an easy one for Harold. It was a brand new release.

"Shirley and Lee," he said matter-of-factly. "Aladdin, 1956, maroon, flip side, *Do You Mean to Hurt Me?"*

None of this carefully accumulated knowledge would do him much good in Palm Springs. What would they know about real music in the sticks? He was going to have to start all over, finding new friends, marking out a new territory. He put on his favorite record of all time, lay down on the bed and closed his eyes.

Tutti Frutti, Little Richard, Specialty, 1955, yellow and white, flip side *I'm Just a Lonely Guy.*

* * *

Loud banging and screaming came from across the hall, muffled only slightly by the slurping grunt of the air cooler. Enid walked out of her bedroom and put her hand on the doorknob, but decided not to go in. After all, he had been through a lot in the last week or so. The hospital, then that awful funeral.

Only a few people had come to pay their last respects. A couple of neighbors, a colleague from the bank, and an old, senile rabbi who was persuaded to conduct the ceremony, although he didn't know Sylvia or Norman. In fact, this was a minor problem, for the rabbi seemed to have only the faintest idea where he was or exactly what he was supposed to be doing.

"Abel<u>stein</u> !" Enid whispered harshly to him as he mumbled in Hebrew what she was sure simply had to be the bar mitzvah service, "not Abel*man*!"

The rabbi didn't pay any attention. Maybe he couldn't hear her over the traffic noise coming from the nearby Hollywood Freeway. Abelman, Abelstein, what does it matter, thought Enid. Rest in peace, Sylvia. Rest in peace, Norman. Rest in peace.

Not far from the small group of mourners, an old woman dressed in black, dragging a young boy by the hand, wandered among the rows of identical white tomb markers set like paving stones into the ground.

"Irving! Where are you, Irving? Where are you?" the woman wailed loudly.

Startled by the cry, the rabbi looked up. He stopped in the

middle of a prayer. Thinking he had finished, he closed his prayer book, shook Harold's hand and walked away. No one stopped him. There seemed little point.

Enid had driven Harold straight back to Palm Springs. He hardly said a word the entire trip. She figured he must still be in shock.

A Temporary Arrangement

Enid Cohen had been in Palm Springs for only a few days before she decided to change her name to Carlson. That was in 1949. She was 26. No one said anything to her, but the hotel or *Inn* as it was called, where she worked as a cocktail waitress, was restricted and she thought it would make life easier not to be too readily identified. She told herself that in any case she would have to change her name when she got married, so what difference did it really make if she did it before? Going from Cohen to Carlson was not much of a compromise, but it was important if she was to get ahead in Palm Springs. Enid wanted very much to get ahead.

Being a cocktail waitress had appealed to her. It was a step up from working at Lockheed assembling aircraft parts, which she had done for three years. Her friends said that all the movie people came to Palm Springs to relax. You could get closer to the right people there than in Los Angeles. Palm Springs was surely the place to be discovered. Discovered, like a gold mine — a Hollywood gold mine. She didn't think much past being discovered. She was a very good-looking woman. All she needed was that one small break. The studio would do the rest. It said so in all the movie magazines. It had to be true.

It didn't work out. The only movie people she ever met were a couple of bit part actors who hung out in the hotel bar telling each other drunken stories. Even they weren't interested in Enid. She found out later that they were homosexuals. That didn't make her feel any better about not being discovered.

Instead of being discovered, she was on her feet for hours, having to smile at the customers' crude remarks, often made to her in front of their wives. Nights were spent fending off pawing hands and politely turning down not-so-politely whispered propositions.

"They're down here to have a little harmless fun," said the manager, solicitously. "Come on, sweetheart, it happens to all the girls. You shouldn't get yourself so upset about it."

It was more of an order than a bit of friendly advice. For weeks she cried herself to sleep. Then she met Archie.

She was with Charlene, the girl with whom she shared a dark, tiny room at the the back of the hotel. It was their day off, and they had gone to the driving range on Highway 111.

"I don't know shit from spit about golf," said Charlene, picking a worn driver out of a barrel by the side of the wooden hut, "but I love to smack these here balls. You gotta picture in your mind them creeps, saying that shit at you behind their hands, grabbing at you. You know what I mean, honey. Right? You got that picture? Good. Well, now you take this club and you put this little ol' white ball down on the ground here, and you think it right into their pants. See it laying up alongside their little ol' shriveled-up peckers and then...."

WHACK! The ball sailed on a high straight arc and disappeared into the sand behind a bullseye with 150 painted in the center.

Enid giggled. She had never had a golf club in her hand. She watched Charlene and tried to copy her. It was hopeless. At first she couldn't hit the ball. When she finally did, it bounced off the tee and rolled ten feet across the sand.

It was Archie who came over and offered to give her some pointers. A week later she gave up her job at the hotel, said good-bye to Charlene and moved out.

Archie Blatt was in his early fifties. He was in the rag trade in St. Louis and had come to Palm Springs to escape the winter, his invalid wife and the consuming angst of his two young teenage daughters. When they were little their crying and whining had driven him crazy, now they filled the house with noisy friends and noisier music. When he complained about it they sulked. They clearly resented his being in his own house. He spent as much time as he could at work or at his club. In Palm Springs he found complete freedom. It was far from all those things which made him so unhappy, and he could be alone with Enid.

"I never really wanted any... you know, kids. 'Who needs the bother at our age,' I said to her. 'We've been living all right, just you and me, for the last fifteen years. I don't want to share you with anyone else. I don't want to start with diapers and all that stuff at forty.' But, Sarah, she was, well you know, she thought if she didn't then she never would... and, anyway, so she had the twins. Thirteen years ago it was. It went wrong, you see, the birth. Complications. I don't know what exactly. Had to have everything out, and then she got depressed and sick and well, so it went on. If only we'd..."

What had once been indifference changed into a fierce hatred of children. For Archie they were destroyers, invaders, another species. He thought when his daughters were grown up and out of his house, maybe then he would like them. But, he confessed to Enid, in his blacker moments he knew they would never grow up and never leave home.

Archie's difficulty with children hadn't bothered Enid. It had never been very important to their relationship. From the beginning she felt completely at ease with him. He was a short, round man with bandy legs. Enid was two inches taller. He was almost totally bald and had the hairiest body she had ever seen. Arms, chest, back, legs were all coated with a dense mat of curly black hair. She thought of him as a small cuddly gorilla. He was kind, paid attention to her, treated her like a lady, and most importantly for Enid, he made her laugh.

The ease and the laughter seemed to be important for Archie as well, almost more so than sex. He was obviously not a ladies' man, which was one reason Enid liked him. When he had picked her up he stumbled self-consciously over his words. He had looked weak-kneed when he asked her to go for a drink and when she agreed to come his relief was audible.

They quickly came to an arrangement. He would rent a small house and send her a check every month. The only thing she had to do was be there when he came out from St. Louis, three, maybe four times a year. What she did the rest of the time, whom she saw, was up to her. Maybe Archie realized that he couldn't hold her if he laid down too many conditions.

"You shouldn't worry, doll," he explained helpfully. "I'll get the accountant to figure out some way to get you down as a tax write-off."

Being a tax write-off didn't make Enid feel any better about

Archie's offer. But, when she thought of the immediate alternatives — the hotel, the dingy room, the succession of men "down to have a little harmless fun", she figured she didn't have anything to lose. She would try it, strictly as a temporary deal, until something better came along.

Nothing better did come along, and more than seven years later she was still in his house, still dependent on the monthly checks from St. Louis. Now she had to figure some way to tell Archie about her nephew's new living arrangements. She was beyond worried. If he hated his own kids, how was he going to react to Harold? Big, inarticulate, noisy Harold.

It was too late in life to go back to waitressing, although if that was really true, why were there so many middle-aged waitresses? Enid prefered not to think about too much. about middle-aged waitresses.

* * *

The music from Harold's room was now much softer.

Deep purple... sun... lingers...

She sat down on her bed, opened the drawer of her bedside table, reached in and took out a pack of Salems. Her record six non-smoking days had ended with the accident. A few more days, she thought, then I'll try to stop again. She tapped out a cigarette and put it in her mouth. She picked up a book of matches from a white bowl full of match books. Chi-Chi, The Doll House, Ruby's Dunes, The Biltmore, and others — Palm Springs' nightlife. She threw the matches and the unlit cigarette on the table, pulled her knees up and hugged them.

What was she going to do about Harold? Do with Harold? After the accident, when it dawned on her that she had inherited him, she dismissed her initial misgivings with the thought that it might actually be nice not to live alone. That thought didn't last very long. As soon as he moved into her house the misgivings returned and when they did they were Haroldly substantial.

The music reminded her that he was there. He was going to be there now all the time, at least for another three years until he got out of high school and maybe after that, living with her, so obviously just across the hall from her bedroom. A stranger sharing her bathroom, invading her house, threatening to derail her life. She felt guilty about thinking of Harold that way, but couldn't help herself. When she touched him, asked him how he was or whether he needed anything, the resentment of his being there threatened to collapse her concerned-aunt's smile. She knew she should like Harold, even love him. These contradictory feelings made Enid feel bad about herself and she was not used to feeling bad about herself.

When he had come to visit with Sylvia and Norman, it had been easy for her. Then she had enjoyed the idea of having a nephew, someone calling her "Aunt Enid". It was like being part of a family. But then they never stayed more than a few days. A permanent Harold was something else.

What the hell did you do with a fifteen-year-old? Enid had no experience with kids. There was school to worry about and clothes, regular meals and a lot of other things she had never wanted to have to think about.

She got up from the bed and went out into the hall. The music was blasting out again. She imagined she could see the door to what until recently had been her dressing room vibrating.

Enid walked into the living room and opened the sliding glass door which led onto the patio. She went out and sat down in a canvas chair by the pool. It was about six o'clock and although the pool was in the shade it was still very hot. She pulled off her slacks and blouse, then after checking to make sure Harold was not around, she undid her bra, took off her panties and slipped naked into the cool water. Everything seemed easier when she was in the pool and could feel the water against her skin. She closed her eyes, floated on her back and thought about Archie.

She never really loved him in the way she had imagined love was going to be. There was no real romance. Although she enjoyed making love with Archie, she had never had a strong physical desire for him. Not in any way could he be considered a sexy man, but he was warm, generous, and amusing — a comfortable man. And, he loved Enid seemingly with unreserved devotion. Even after seven years he acted as if he was genuinely overwhelmed, grateful that such a woman should be his woman. Archie Blatt's woman. She laughed when he called her that one night. Until then she had never thought of herself as "Archie Blatt's woman."

Over the years she had had a few affairs while he was in St. Louis, but she always ended them before he came back. It wasn't just the money, she never found anyone she liked to be with as much as Archie. She had settled for that. Now everything was up in the air.

Would he stop her money? Throw her out? How much did he love her? It would have to be a great deal if Harold was put on the scales. And all she had was about $700 in her bank account. The house was rented, even the car belonged to Archie's company. Enid felt very vulnerable. It wasn't the first time.

When it all started with Archie she hadn't worried too much about being kept. It seemed romantic, exciting, something out of a steamy Southern novel. Anyway, if Archie got fed up and tossed her out she wouldn't have been any worse off than before. Within a few months, however, complete dependence and lack of security started to nag at her. Also there wasn't much for her to do in Palm Springs. She didn't really know anyone except Charlene. She started going to the public library on Palm Canyon Drive. The books didn't help. Enid was not a reader.

In the same block as the library was the Plaza, a Spanish colonial-style arcade of shops put up just before the war. She found a part-time job there in a small gift shop. The pay wasn't great, but it was all hers, it got her out of the house and it filled in some of the spaces. Archie hadn't liked it.

"Hey, babe, if I'm not giving you enough money, just say the word. It's no problem."

"It's not that, Archie."

"What then?"

She hedged, not wanting him to guess the real reason.

"I just need a little something of my own is all. Something to do."

Her allowance was increased. She quit her job and he persuaded her to take up golf.

"After all, babe," he laughed, "that's what got us together in the first place."

He paid for lessons and tried to join Tamarisk, a new golf club and the only one in the area which accepted Jews. They never got past the membership committee. The sister of the wife of someone on the committee lived in St. Louis and knew the Blatts and someone else knew about Enid. Tamarisk Country Club was a very straight set-up. Archie got a polite letter: "We are sorry, but under the circumstances..."

"What a place!" he exclaimed, throwing the letter on the couch, "Even the goddamn Jews don't want us!"

They were forced to play at O'Donnell, the public course. Archie made the best of it.

"Listen," he said. "Maybe they did us a favor, babe. O'Donnell is a nice course and it's right here in town, not like Tamarisk or Thunderbird way to hell and gone out there in the desert. Sure, you could walk there if you wanted. And we don't have to worry about those stuck-up bastards and all that country club stuff. Yeah. They did us a big-time favor."

To her surprise, especially after her performance at the driving range, Enid discovered that she was a natural golfer. Within a few months she was going around the course in the mid-80s. Archie was delighted. She made new friends and spent a lot of time at the O'Donnell clubhouse. She met people there who invited her and Archie to the Racquet Club. The Racquet Club catered to movie people, and as long as he could pay the membership fee no one was concerned about exactly who Archie's wife was. They joined and Enid took up tennis. Her days filled with activity, and it became easy not to think too much about the future. It would take care of itself.

She wasn't so sure about that anymore.

But Archie wasn't due back until the end of September, more than two months. Maybe it would all work out. He was a nice guy. He might surprise her and even like Harold. She pushed her arms slowly through the water, letting that idea settle. It didn't. Who was she kidding? Even for a person who loved kids Harold would be hard work. After all, what was to like, *really* like, about her nephew? In the first place he was well over six feet, more than six inches taller than Archie. That wasn't a great start. Added to that, and even leaving out the death of his parents, Harold seemed to be having a particularly rocky adolescence. He was awkward, morose, overweight, and could shower more often then he did. A teenage nightmare. And the music he played! Archie was strictly an Eddie Fisher-Frank Sinatra-Broadway Show Tunes person. She turned over and began to swim a vigorous crawl.

* * *

Harold stood by the sliding glass door in the living room watching his aunt. He had a painful erection. It was the first time he had actually seen a completely naked woman in the flesh. Sure, there was *Playboy* and there were those pictures in nudist magazines that got passed around at school, the pages wrinkled and greasy, the photos always frustratingly just out of focus, vaginas and penises airbrushed out, as if they didn't exist. Harold knew better. He spent a good deal of time wondering about vaginas.

Outside

Enid was increasingly concerned about her nephew. He had never been a talkative child, but now he had withdrawn almost completely. All day he stayed in the house playing his records or watching television. It was a week since the funeral and he hadn't mentioned his parents. In fact, he rarely said anything and showed no sign of wanting to get out of the house.

"Harold darling, it isn't normal for a big boy like you to sit inside all day. You should go out. See the town, maybe meet some kids or something. There's a nice boy about your age who lives just up the road here. I've seen him go by on his bike. You should go over and introduce yourself. It's another month or so before school starts again. You want to make some friends, don't you, darling?"

Enid was by the kitchen sink washing the breakfast dishes. She was wearing very short white shorts and a low-cut halter top. Every few seconds she glanced over her shoulder to make sure Harold was paying attention. He was, to the way her bottom moved as she scrubbed whatever it was she was holding, to her breasts, exposed almost to the nipples when she bent over. He tried not to stare, but couldn't help himself.

Her body was endlessly fascinating. At one moment he was swamped with sexual desire, not for his aunt, of course not, but for the separate parts of her body. In the next moment he was drained by his revulsion. After all, she was his aunt, she was almost twenty years older than him, and he didn't actually want to touch her. He didn't even like her very much.

He had never seen his mother naked. Both his parents were meticulously circumspect about not exposing their bodies. Bedroom and bathroom doors were always firmly locked.

"Harold! How many times do I have to tell you to close the

bathroom door when you urinate?"

"Are you listening to me, Harold?"

He quickly shifted his eyes downward as his aunt turned her head.

"Yeah, Aunt Enid."

"What do you mean, 'Yeah, Aunt Enid'? Come on!"

He shuffled his feet back and forth under the table. He could feel his face reddening.

"It's just that you can't just go up to someone like that, you know. It's..."

"What are you waiting for, a formal invitation?"

"You don't understand. You know..."

"I don't know, darling. I really don't. Maybe I should come out there and introduce you?"

He looked up in genuine alarm.

"No, Jesus, Aunt Enid!"

At this point his mother would have shouted at him. Aunt Enid laughed.

"OK, OK, darling. Don't worry, I won't embarrass you. You do what you want."

She dried her hands on the sides of her shorts, crossed the room, bent down and hugged him. There was no escape.

* * *

Aunt Enid's house was in the north end of Palm Springs. It was only a few blocks from the center of town, but in the early August heat the walk seemed much longer. There were no sidewalks and Harold had to trudge through the soft sand by the side of the road. After a hundred yards his legs hurt. By the time he got to Palm Canyon Drive he was gasping. The sweat dripped down his sides and pooled in the creases of his stomach. His aunt had insisted he wear one of her straw hats. The straw was long and carefully frayed all around the brim. It made him look like a beachcomber. He felt stupid. He wanted to turn back, but knew he probably wouldn't make it. He needed a cold Coke. It was better to keep moving.

He had decided to venture out to search for a record store. The chances of finding a place with the music he liked were slim, but buying records was Harold's major passion, and after more than a week away from the racks of new 45s in their crisp paper wrappers he was getting restless.

Harold had been initiated into music by Alvin Harper. When Harold was thirteen, Alvin and his mother had moved into the downstairs apartment. He was about twenty-five years old and had been disfigured and blinded in Korea. He stayed in all day with the drapes closed playing music. Harold hadn't been able to figure out any of the words, only the thump of the bass came through the floor. It drove his mother crazy. She forced her husband to go and tell whoever it was to turn down the noise or they would complain to the landlord. It was then they found out about Alvin.

"Hey, boy! I hear y'all stepping by that door now. Y'all come over here. I ain't gonna harm you, little peckerwood that you is. No need to be afeared of ol' Alvin."

There was every need in the world. Raised scars sliced across Alvin's face. One scar was partially hidden behind dark glasses, the other had taken a lump out of his chin and curled up a corner of his mouth, giving him a perpetual sneer. Alvin was built like a scarecrow, his clothes hanging loosely from bony shoulders and thin arms. His mutilated face and his stiff-legged blind-man's walk terrified Harold.

It wasn't until years later that Harold would think how strange it was that a white Southerner should be so caught up with Negro music. At the time he had no experience with either Southerners or Negroes or music and he took it all as it came.

How it came was hard, raw and mainly from the Delta, for Alvin Harper was a purist. For him John Lee Hooker, Lightnin' Hopkins and Muddy Waters were latecomers. He tolerated them, but Robert Johnson was his god. Harold spent hours in Alvin's apartment being schooled in the finer points of the blues, listening to scratchy 78 rpm recordings of Tampa Red, Kokomo Arnold, Lonnie Johnson, Black Boy Shine, Pinetop Burks, and others — Blind This, Big Mouth That, Three-Fingers Someone Else.

His mother didn't approve of him hanging out with Alvin. To begin with he was far too old for Harold. Also, Alvin was virtually an illiterate, and that could be nothing but a bad influence on her impressionable son, who was already having enough problems at school. And, of course, there was the music. Sylvia Abelstein violently detested the music that leaked noisily into their lives from the apartment below.

"Jungle noise, Harold. Nothing but uncivilized jungle noise. Thump, thump, thump! Shout, shout, shout! Music? Give me a break, please."

At first he hadn't really cared for it much either, but sandwiched between Alvin's insistent proselytizing and his mother's persistent hostility he soon acquired a taste for the blues, although he had little more than a hazy understanding of what broken hearts or bad women or babies being gone or mojo hands or getting up soon in the morning were all about. When he asked, Alvin either told him stuff that was even more incomprehensible or laughed wildly and shook his head, sending thick strings of spit flying in all directions. Harold soon stopped asking such questions.

Alvin bought his records at dingy hole-in-the-wall shops off Hollywood Boulevard. They all seemed to be called Moe's or Jim's or Sam's. Harold went with him and discovered a whole new world. But, it wasn't Alvin's world of treasured 78s, of obscure Mississippi Delta blues men. It was the new 45s of B.B. King, the Ravens, Bo Diddley, the Penguins, Lloyd Price, LaVern Baker, Muddy Waters — stuff he had never heard on the radio, that is until he found KRKD, LA's only Negro station. The rolling stomp of Fats Domino's piano on *The Fat Man*, the joyous shriek from Little Richard, the Wolf's growl, the echoed whine of Elmore James's guitar all hit him in places where he hadn't known he had places. He figured that was all the understanding he needed.

"You just ain't a gonna get the same sound on these little biddy things. Shit, child, they ain't never replace the good ol' 78."

He also didn't approve of Harold's choice of music. According to Alvin that wouldn't last either.

Harold crossed to the west side of the street to get into the shade. It helped a little. He walked down towards the center of town looking for somewhere to get a drink. He passed a place called Desert Dates, a men's clothing store, a barbershop, a children's shoe store. All of them had sun-bloated brown paper covering the inside of their windows.

SORRY, CLOSED FOR THE SUMMER.

He could see why. The street was virtually empty. A few cars, fewer people. As he passed a wooden bench, an old guy with a long white beard, wearing torn and faded shorts and leather sandals, raised his walking stick in greeting. Harold was too surprised to respond. He noticed that the old man had on a straw hat with a fringe. He walked on a little faster.

Finally he found a drug store that was open. There were a few people sitting in the red plastic booths. He went inside, sat down at the counter and ordered a Coke. The jukebox played *Tutti Frutti* by Pat Boone. It summed up Palm Springs for Harold. One of the greatest songs ever written, he thought. Maybe the greatest song ever written. Pat Fucking Boone! A wave of despair swept over him. He took off his hat, rested his soft arms on the Formica counter and let cool air blow over him. It was a very, very long way from LA.

"A real hot one today," said the waitress, as she put the glass down in front of him.

She was bleached blond, sixteen, maybe seventeen, with a mouth full of orthodontal steel.

"Yeah...thanks," Harold replied uneasily, looking down at the floor.

Girls his own age made him nervous, even more nervous than Aunt Enid did. He sipped the Coke, letting the crushed ice melt slowly on his tongue.

"You down on vacation or what?" she asked, leaning forward and squinting nearsightedly at Harold.

There was a slight gap between the top buttons of her white uniform. He could see the edge of her bra and imagined the roundness of a breast. He disengaged his eyes and concentrated on the silver and green malted milk machine behind her. He knew he was blushing. There was nothing he could do about it.

"Um, Uh...No. Just moved here."

"Neat, ain't he?"

"Who, I..."

"Pat Boone, silly. You know, the singer."

She pointed at the juke box selector on the counter.

Wop Ba Ba Lo Ba and a...

The voice was smooth, white, cozy, everything the song shouldn't be. Harold felt sick. The long walk, the heat and now Pat Boone. It was too much.

"Are you OK or what?"

He nodded, put two dimes on the counter and pushed himself up from the stool. He felt his weight like never before. With some effort he moved towards the door.

"Hey," the girl called after him, "you forgot your hat."

Two men sitting in a booth by the door turned to look at him. One of them was wearing a battered cowboy hat. His small eyes were very close together, his skin like overlapping slabs of sun-dried meat. He gave Harold a lipless smirk. Harold saw a thin forked tongue flick out darkly between the man's lips. Over by the counter the girl had the straw hat in her hand and was waving it in the air. The hat was gigantic. Bloated. Surely he couldn't wear it.

Got a gal named Daisy, she almost drives me crazy.

Harold turned and stumbled out into the street.

* * *

She sat on her bed and looked across at her reflection in the full-length mirror on the closet door. Not bad for a woman pushing thirty-five, she thought. She felt her thighs. The muscle tone was still there. Her chin was firm, her neck taut. Maybe it was marriage that did it to the others, having kids. So many of the women she met at the club seemed to have let go. Not that they didn't take care of themselves. In fact, most of them seemed to do little else. They dieted, spent hours at the beauty parlor, bought expensive clothes. It was just that they didn't have the vitality any more, the fine edge. Enid prided herself on being able to maintain a fine edge.

She rubbed the white cream into her hands, added a little more and spread it on her arms and her legs. She loved being tan, but in the last few years she had noticed how the sun dried out her skin. But nothing was for nothing, she supposed and there was no way she was not going to sit in the sun. Being brown all over was too much part of her. It made her feel healthy. She also thought it made her look younger. Younger was becoming increasingly important for Enid.

For reasons she didn't understand, having Harold around the house had made her more conscious not only of her age but of her life. By doing that, he had accomplished in a week what her sister had been unable to do in more than seven years of constant nagging.

Sylvia had always disapproved of her younger sister, even when they were kids. She thought Enid was irresponsible and frivolous and immoral.

"How can you take the man's money like that?"

"You take Norman's money, don't you?"

"But he's my husband, Enid. My husband. This Arnold guy..."

"Archie. His name is Archie."

"Archie then. This guy, he's married for Christ sake!"

"So's Norman," laughed Enid.

Sylvia didn't think that was funny.

Now they were both dead. Buried beside the Hollywood Freeway. Poor Sylvia. All those years being so careful to do the right thing. Enid wept for her dead sister.

After a while she got up and went into the bathroom. Her mascara had run. She took a tissue and cleaned her face, blew her nose.

She walked out to the living room, sat down and turned on the TV. Jack Baily's round, moustached faced filled the screen. His hair was slick and plastered down. He was smiling. *Queen for a Day*. She hated the program, but couldn't not watch. It was hypnotically compelling, like an elaborately-ritual execution.

"And, Mrs.Thomas, will you tell the studio audience why you want to be Queen for a Day!"

Mrs. Thomas had some story to tell. Was there really that much pain in the world? By the time she finished, Mrs. Thomas was in tears and so was Enid.

She knew she would have to call Archie soon and tell him her new story. It was going to be difficult to explain everything to him over the phone. Her stomach went queasy when she tried to imagine the conversation.

"It's my husband, Mr. Baily, he hasn't been very well these last few years. He hasn't been able to work regular like. And we have five children. Helen, she's the youngest..."

"Yes, Mrs. Botham. And exactly what has been the matter with Mr. Botham?"

She would also have to have a serious talk with Harold. Her sister had been very anxious about Harold's lack of progress at high school. Would he be alright at the local high school? She didn't know anything about schools. She would have to find out about that. And then of course, there was Archie. Always back to Archie. She was not only going to have to explain Harold to Archie, she was going to have to explain Archie to Harold.

"And candidate number five, who wants a new stove."

Wild applause sent the needle on the applause-meter swinging all the way over to the left. No washing machine for Mrs. Thomas. Tough luck.

Enid reached over and turned off the set. The picture imploded softly, fading to a small white dot in the center of the screen.

* * *

"Hey partner, you still alive down there?"

Harold opened his eyes. It was a few seconds before he could focus. A face shaded by a cowboy hat, peered down at him. He remembered the snakeman in the drug store, thought for a moment he must still be in the drug store. He wasn't. He was lying on his back in the sand. A few feet away was a horse, its long neck stretched out, mouth moving along the ground by the side of an adobe wall searching for something to eat. It was very quiet except for the swishing whisper of the horse's browsing lips and the loud buzzing of flies. One landed near his nose. He reached up and brushed it away. He couldn't understand why the horse was there or exactly why he was there or even where "there" was. The last thing he remembered clearly was Aunt Enid's straw hat and Pat Boone's singing *Tutti Frutti.*

"Where you live at?"

Harold sat up. He was dizzy, sick to his stomach, and his face was burning hot.

"Shit! Oh shit," he moaned.

"You don't look so good. Gotta get you outta the sun. Come on, let me help you up."

Two strong arms lifted him onto his feet. He felt unsteady and held on to the boy's arm.

The boy was about Harold's age, maybe a little older. Tall and thin. Cowboy boots, Levis, silver belt buckle, checked western shirt with triangle flap pockets and mother-of-pearl buttons, and, of course, a cowboy hat.

"Looking for a record shop. Everything was closed. Couldn't even see in the damn windows... Fucking Pat Boone!"

The boy laughed.

"Yeah, he ain't much to write home about, is he. For sure he ain't no Hank Williams."

The boy paused, kicked at the sand with the toe of his boot.

"Yeah poor ol' Hank Williams."

Harold nodded. Yes, he thought, poor old Hank Williams. He had never heard of Hank Williams. He began to giggle. Poor old Hank Williams.

The boy looked at Harold with concern. He shook his head.

"You are sure one sunblasted son-of-a-bitch. I gotta git you home. Where is it you live at, cowboy?"

"Poor old Hank Williams," muttered Harold to himself. "Poor old Hank Williams."

"Come on now, where is it you live at?"

Harold smiled at his new friend.

"Abelstein, Harold Abelstein."

"Ha! That right?"

"Abelstein," Harold repeated slow and deliberate, "Harold Abelstein."

"I got you. So, Harold Abelstein, what the Sam hell am I going to do with you?"

He thought a minute and then led Harold over to the horse.

"Can you ride?"

Harold stared uncomprehendingly at the horse and then at the boy.

"Yeah, I suppose not. Can you walk?"

Harold managed a nod.

"Right, come on I'll take you back to the stables. It ain't far. You can wait there out of the sun 'til your brains unscramble."

They started down the road, Harold leaning heavily on the boy.

"You ain't no lightweight, are you, Harold Abelstein?"

About a hundred yards down the road a woman in a bikini came running out of a house. It was Aunt Enid. She had been getting a drink in the kitchen, staring out the window when she saw the two boys and the horse.

As she rushed at them the horse shied, pulling powerfully on the reins. To keep control of the horse, the boy had to let go of Harold. Unsupported he staggered towards his aunt. His face was bright red. His eyes were half closed.

"Harold? Harold darling! What's the matter, Harold? What's happened to you? Oh my God!... Where's your hat?"

"I found him just up there is all," said the boy, staring at Enid's breasts while pointing back up the road.

Harold grinned stupidly at his aunt.

"Poor old Hank Williams," he said, as he fell forward.

Enid tried to grab him but he was much too heavy for her. He collapsed through her arms and landed in an untidy pile at her feet.

Enid looked down at her nephew. This is my fault, she said to herself. I nagged him about going out, so he went out and now look what's happened. Maybe I wanted it to happen so as to punish him for being here. No, I couldn't want that, could I?

She pulled the straps of her bikini higher up on her shoulders.

Harold was too heavy to carry. They had to drag him. The heels of his shoes left two very deep tracks in the gravel at the front of Enid's house. It couldn't be helped.

Sort Of Telling It Like It Is

"We must have a talk, Harold darling."

He was watching television. It was his one sure way out of Palm Springs. Harold would settle for just about anything: *Father Knows Best*, *The Adventures of Ozzie and Harriet*, although he had to draw the line at *Oh Suzanna*. Gail Storm made him puke.

"Please, Harold, just a few minutes."

Reluctantly he looked away from the television. Enid reached over and turned off the sound. She sat down in a chair next to Harold.

It was two days since his sunstroke. The blisters and strips of peeling skin made it look a lot worse, but the swelling had gone down and his face didn't hurt so much any more.

"How are you feeling, dear?"

She reached over and patted his knee. He shifted uneasily, still half watching the flickering screen, trying to figure out what was being said. Why did she have to bother him now?

"OK, thanks. I'm OK."

"That's good, darling. Harold, please... Please, dear, pay attention. We haven't really talked about things since the funeral. You can watch that later."

How could she say that? He knew there was no way he could watch it later. It would be finished later and he would never know what happened. He sighed and turned to face his aunt.

"That's better, darling. Thank you. I know things have been difficult, Harold. I know that. But, we must have a little heart to heart about the future. OK? ... Harold?"

He stared down between his feet.

"The last time I talked to Sylvia, to your mother, she said you were having a lot of trouble at school. Is that right, dear?"

"Not really trouble," he answered, continuing to study the floor.

"I see."

Enid knew that getting through to Harold was going to be hard work. But, she felt she had at least to try for her sister's sake. Maybe for her own as well. If she tried harder with Harold it might make her feel less guilty about the uncharitable thoughts she had about him.

"And what are you without a college diploma these days?" Sylvia had asked her sister, bemoaning Harold's latest disaster at school.

"A nobody?"

"A nobody. Right, a nobody. At least we agree about something, Enid."

Neither of the Cohen girls had had much of an education. First Sylvia, then Enid had to leave high school to support their mother. Their father had disappeared in 1933. He left their house in the Bronx one morning saying he was going to look for work. He didn't come back. They'd never heard from him.

"Please, Harold, we must talk to each other. Talk honestly. Your mother said she was worried that you were doing so badly in school. Were you getting bad report cards or something?"

A chill settled in his stomach. Report cards. He had almost succeeded in forgetting about report cards, about school. Somehow he had assumed that all that had been obliterated by the accident, together with his parents and his life in Los Angeles. When Aunt Enid mentioned report cards, he realized that he hadn't thought it out very well. Like lots of other things in his life, he hadn't wanted to think about it. He still didn't.

"What do you call this, Harold? What?"

His mother stood by the table in the dining room glaring down at him, holding his latest report card out in front of her as if it was a quarantine notice.

"My report card?"

"Don't be such a wise guy, Harold. I know it's your report card. But, look at what it says. Look at these grades, if you can call them grades. D's. All D's. In Math a D. In English a D. In History..."

"OK, Mom! OK!"

"What do you mean, OK? OK? It's anything but OK, young

man. ...In History a D. In Spanish a D. In..."

"I'm sure Harold gets the message, dear."

"Message, Norman? Exactly what message are we talking about here?"

"You know what I mean, Sylvia. Come on."

She ignored her husband and turned back to Harold.

"In Spanish a D. A..."

"Mom, you already said that."

"Harold! In Geography a D. In PE a D. How did you manage that? PE a D!"

"I don't like to do gym is all."

"And, I suppose you don't like to do English, or History, or Spanish, or any of the other subjects? Is that it? This is worse than last time. I remember a couple of C's last time. Harold?"

"Sylvia, this isn't getting us anywhere. You're just getting yourself upset."

"You want to handle this, Norman? Do you? As I remember it, you were going to have a man-to-man talk with him after the last report card. So what happened? ...Well?"

"It's not that easy..."

"*Bubkas* is what happened. Absolutely nothing. In fact, it's getting worse."

"He has some problems, Sylvia. We..."

"I'll say he has some problems, but nothing compared to the problems he's going to have if he doesn't start to work harder. What do you think you're going to do in life without a college diploma? Without a high school diploma, for Christ sake! Harold? Huh? Look at your father. If he had had the opportunity to go to college..."

"Sylvia, for God sake!"

"It's not true, Norman? It wouldn't have been easier?"

"Sure, maybe it would, but that doesn't have anything to do with Harold."

"Well, if it doesn't, I don't know what does."

She slammed the yellow card down on the table, leaned forward until her face was inches from her son's.

"So, what are you going to do? What?"

Harold didn't have an answer. He hadn't thought about it.

Sort Of Telling It Like It Is

School had always been there, and Harold had always found it hard going. Most of the time he just wasn't interested. He figured that school was one of those things adults did to children. It had to be put up with. So, Harold put up with it. Despite what it might seem like, he knew it couldn't last forever.

"Harold?"

"Yes, Aunt Enid."

"Report cards, Harold? Bad report cards?"

"Yeah?"

"Harold, help me out here just a little, will you? OK, OK, look, you don't like school, right?"

Harold nodded.

"Fine. Why don't you like school?"

His mother had never asked him that. He thought about it.

"I don't know, it's just, you know, sort of boring like. And, um we do this stuff, and it's, you know..."

"Boring?"

"Yeah."

Enid was struggling through heavy mud.

Harold's eyes began to slip back towards the television. He tried to read the actors' lips, but they were too far away from the camera.

"Listen, darling. Please listen. How would it be if I sent you to a nice private school here in Palm Springs?"

As soon as she said it, she realized she hadn't thought it through. For too long she had been around women at the club who didn't have to worry about money. But, how was she going to afford it? She didn't even know how much it cost. If only his parents had left something for Harold. They hadn't. For some reason, Norman had apparently never got around to taking out a life insurance policy. There was only what she could get for their furniture, a few hundred dollars. It wouldn't go far. She would have to ask Archie. That wasn't a pleasant prospect. Not only was he going to be asked to share his house with Harold, he was going to be asked to support him.

"Huh?" Harold grunted in surprise.

For the first time he looked directly at his aunt.

"That's better, dear. Now listen. A couple of the girls at the club send their children to a school near here called Date Grove. They have small classes, lots of individual attention. It would be nice for you, Harold darling, it really would. What do you think?"

He didn't see what difference it would make, school was school.

"Sure, Aunt Enid, that'd be OK, but what about the money? Doesn't something like that cost a lot?"

At one point his parents had been so desperate that they thought of sending Harold to a military school. But it was much too expensive. Harold was glad that his parents didn't have the money. The last thing he wanted to do was go to a military school.

"It could be a problem, darling, but I think we could find the money. I've got a friend who I'm sure would help us."

She wasn't at all sure. He might help them both into the street.

"Oh, well that's fine then," said Harold turning his attention back to the television.

There was a commercial for used cars. A man wearing a checked coat was pointing to the price sticker on a '56 Thunderbird.

The heart to heart was over. Enid reached over and turned up the volume.

"Low down payments, 24 easy monthly payments. Come on down tomorrow, folks. We're at the corner of Central and the Slauson. We're open seven days a week."

"Goodnight, Harold."

His eyes remained fixed to the screen. After being forced to trek across the desert he was not going leave the oasis now.

"Yeah... goodnight, Aunt Enid."

* * *

Enid opened the drawer of the bedside table to look for a new emery board. The one she was using was almost smooth. The pack of Salems lay there waiting for her. She pushed them to one side and picked out the emery board. She began to shape her nails. Tomorrow she would put on a new coat of nail polish. A new color — Midnight Red. She thought she might even do her toes if there was time. Maybe go out and play a few holes of golf later in the afternoon, when it was cooler. Then she remembered what month it was and that none of her club friends would be there. They all had husbands or other homes to go to when the summer closed in. They had flown north. She would call Charlene.

There were muffled voices from the living room. Harold was still watching. TV and records. Since his abortive journey into town that was about it for Harold. More so than before. And, of course, there was eating. The kid could eat. When she had been on her own, Enid ate out most of the time. Now she was having to go to the supermarket and do the cooking. She didn't mind it as much as she thought she would. It was a change and she found she actually enjoyed cooking, even for Harold. He wasn't picky. He ate everything she put in front of him, most of the time without looking up from the plate.

On the whole, however, Harold was not a joy to be with. She had to admit that. Getting two words out of him was a struggle and when they came out they were painfully inarticulate. But, she knew she would have to be patient. It was, after all, only two weeks since the accident. He'd been with her for ten days. It would take time for him to adjust, time for them to adjust to each other. And, she was his only blood relation. For that matter, he was her only blood relation, her entire family. There had to be some mileage in that. She tried to think about exactly how much.

The toilet flushed. The heavy tread of footsteps, a door being closed. She counted the seconds. Eight, nine, ten... Then the music started. It was as if something terrible would happen if he had a noiseless moment. Were all kids like this? She didn't know. Kids had always been for other people. Crying, smelly, and demanding when they were little, in the way when they got older. She'd never wanted any of her own and here she was with Harold. She laughed. A real prize package.

She got up from the bed, opened the door and went out into the hall.

"Please, darling, can you turn it down just a little? It is after 12 o'clock."

Harold didn't answer, but he did lower the volume. She went back into her room and lay down again. As long as it wasn't too loud the music didn't really bother her, but Archie was going to be a different story.

"It's the goddamn crickets, babe. Can't you hear the little bastards? Out there hissing themselves stupid. Jesus! I thought it was supposed to be quiet in the desert. How am I supposed to sleep with that racket going on?"

Crickets. Archie was worried about crickets. He had to wear earplugs to get to sleep. What chance was he going to have with Harold's music?

She looked at the phone by the side of the bed. Tomorrow. It could wait a while longer. She would definitely call Archie tomorrow.

* * *

"It is after twelve o'clock."

Through the door and over the Fat Man's music Aunt Enid sounded like his mother. The same voice. His mother had yelled a lot more. Still, it was early days.

He pulled a record out of one of the boxes. Joe Turner, *Shake, Rattle and Roll*, Atlantic, 1954, yellow and black. He had bought it at that place off of Vine Street. Alvin had put him on to the music.

"Shee-it, Harold-boy, it's those white boys making the money with that stuff. Now you just listen to this. I know y'all like this heavy beat stuff. But then you wanna listen to the real gin-u-wine sound."

Harold liked the sound, he liked it a lot and long arguments followed at school over the relative merits of Bill Haley and Big Joe Turner. Most of his friends had never heard of Joe Turner or Lowell Fulson, Elmore James, Johnny Watson or any of the others. Until he brought the record to school, they wouldn't believe that Big Mama Thornton, a Negro woman, had actually recorded *Hound Dog* four years before Elvis. Peacock, 1952, red and silver, flip side *Night Mare*. For most of the other kids it was all Bill Haley, Elvis or for the real retards, Tab Hunter, Paul Anka, and Pat Boone. Elvis had been OK up until *Love Me Tender*, but Pat Boone!

He slipped the record back in the box. J. Turner right behind I. Turner.

The Fats Domino record finished, the arm lifted and returned to the rest, the turntable stopped.

Harold couldn't understand how people survived the summers in Palm Springs. It was almost one in the morning and it was still baking hot. There was no air to breathe. He took off his clothes, put on his pajamas and turned off the light.

There was a full moon. Outside everything was a soft blue. From where he lay he could look out the window and see the thin arm of an ocotillo cactus, a telegraph pole and a slice of the big mountain that rose up immediately to the west of the town. He thought it all looked much better at night.

Private school. What was that going to be like? "Lots of individual attention." That could be trouble. Once in a while a teacher at Fairfax had yelled at him, but most of the time they didn't bother and that was fine with Harold. He didn't want anything to do with individual attention.

In the moonlight the heavy-petaled roses on the walls looked like faces. Hundreds of dark faces. All staring at him. All giving him individual attention. He closed his eyes.

* * *

The phone rang next to her bed. She turned away, pulled the pillow over her head and tried to ignore the insistent noise. The ringing continued. It followed her under the pillow and into her sleep. Finally, with eyes still closed she fumbled on the table for the receiver. She put it to her ear and listened. Over the crackle on the line was the indistinct echoing voice announcing something over a loudspeaker.

"Hello?" she said, her voice husky with sleep, her eyes shut.

"That will be one dollar and twenty-five cents for the first three minutes, please.'

There was a pause.

"Hello, babe, howya doing?"

"Archie?"

"Yeah. Sorry to wake you up so early. I wanted to talk to you."

She opened her eyes and looked at the clock. It was half past five. Archie never called that early. Something had to be wrong. Enid pulled herself awake. She sat up in bed.

"You there, Enid?"

"Sure, darling, I'm here. What's the matter?"

"Nothing, sweetheart. Nothing's the matter. Only something's come up with one of our people in Mexico and I've got to go down there for a week or so to straighten things out. In fact, I'm at the airport right now. On my way back I thought I'd come through LA and then fly down and see you. Spend some time. How about it? And, there's a few little things we gotta talk over."

Her stomach fluttered. What could Archie have in mind? He sounded friendly enough. No hint of bad news in his voice. Still, what he said made her apprehensive.

"What 'little things' do we have to talk over, Archie?"

"Can't really tell you about it over the phone, babe. Don't worry about it, I'll be there soon enough and we can discuss it then."

"Archie, don't tease me, please."

"Hey, I'm not teasing, sweetheart, honest I'm not. I can't wait to see you."

"Me too," said Enid. "It would be just marvelous, Archie darling. But, I didn't expect you for another month or two. You know, when it gets a little cooler."

"What's the matter, babe," he laughed. "You got something going on there I shouldn't know about?"

"You know better than that, Archie. Come on now."

"Only kidding, doll. You know me, always a joke."

"Sure, Archie. I know you."

"So how's every little thing with you, babe?"

Now, thought Enid. I could just let it slip into the conversation. She saw Archie standing by a pay phone in the airport, lots of people walking back and forth, him looking at his watch, thinking about getting on the plane. Was it really the best time to tell him about Harold? To try to explain it all. Maybe not.

"Great. Everything's just great."

"You don't sound so sure about it."

"I only just got up, Archie. I'm still a little dozy."

"Yeah, sure thing. I'm sorry, honey. Listen, they just called my plane. I gotta run. I'll drop you a note from Mexico. Tell you when I'm arriving."

Only then did it occur to Enid that Archie was about to disappear. How would she get in touch with him in Mexico? There would be no way to tell him about anything before he arrived in Palm Springs.

"Archie, listen, darling, I've got to..."

"Please deposit another seventy-five cents for the next three minutes."

"Operator, please," Enid shouted down the phone. "I'll pay..."

There was a distant click. The phone went dead. She'd left it too late. Archie was on his way.

* * *

He was in the corridor at high school. Metal lockers on either side. An acre of green linoleum floor. No one else was there. The bell was ringing for the end of class, but it was too quiet. No running feet, no shouting, no nothing. The bell rang again. Harold woke up.

He was facing the wall next to the bed. A couple of inches away was a large red rose. Eyes half shut, he tried to transform the rose into something else. It wouldn't change. The phone rang. It sounded particularly loud in the quiet house. The cooler hadn't been switched on yet. He rolled over. Every morning he somehow expected them to be gone. Every morning they were there waiting for him. Last night's moonlight faces — morning roses. Surrounding, suffocating him. Another ring. The walls of the room enveloped him as if he were caught up in the soft lining of a woman's bathrobe. Aunt Enid had said she would get him new wallpaper or have someone paint the walls. Today he would definitely have to ask her about it.

Again the phone rang. Now he was fully awake. He sat up in bed, looked out the window. Only the top third of the mountain was lit by the sun. A door slammed somewhere in the house. He looked at his watch. It was 5:30 in the morning. His stomach tightened. Something bad had happened. It was much too early for good news. He had had all the bad news he imagined there was. What more ?

Aunt Enid was in the bathroom. The squeak from the medicine cabinet door, the toilet seat being put down, the rustle of the shower curtain, water running. She would be in there for at least half an hour. First a long shower, then all the make-up, and whatever else she did to herself. Harold couldn't wait. He had to pee. The more he thought about it, heard the water splashing, the more overwhelming was the urge. His penis was painfully stretched in a full-bladder morning-piss hard-on. Discomfort filled up all his space, driving out worry about the phone call.

After fifteen minutes he couldn't stand the pressure any longer. He went outside and peed in the oleander bushes which lined the fence near the swimming pool. As he came back into the house, Enid was just emerging from the bathroom wrapped in a large green towel. When she saw an unexpected Harold stumbling through from the backyard she screamed. Harold replied with a startled shout of his own. They stood very still for a moment eyeing each other. Then they both laughed. It was the first time Enid could remember Harold laughing since he came to live with her. She smiled at him.

"Harold darling, you gave me such a fright," she said, pulling the towel tight around her body.

"Are you alright, dear?"

"Yeah, I'm OK."

"Why were you outside just now?"

"I had to pee, and..."

She smiled at him.

"Of course. It's just that it's so early I didn't expect to see you up."

"It was the phone woke me."

At the mention of the word "phone" her smile broadened and then cracked.

"Yes, I'm sorry about that, it's just that..."

She sat down heavily on a hard-backed chair and began to sob. Her shoulders shook and the towel started to slip. Harold watched, trying to divorce his fascination with her slowly emerging breasts from his disquiet about her crying.

He had been right, the early phone call had been bad news. Where would he have to go now? Who would take care of him? Self-pity started to close in.

"I'm sorry, Harold. I'll be OK in a minute."

He couldn't bring himself to ask her what was wrong. If he sat very still maybe it would pass. He sat very still.

"Let me get dressed and then we can talk. OK, darling?"

Clearly it was not going to pass.

* * *

"No thanks, Aunt Enid, I don't like coffee."'

"Of course, dear, I forgot. I'm sorry."

They sat facing each other at the dining room table. Harold pushed a few stray corn flakes around the sides of his bowl with a spoon. Enid stirred her coffee.

Archie was going to arrive unprepared. Enid thought the least she had better do was prepare Harold. That way she would only have one of them to worry about when the plane landed.

"Harold dear, there is someone coming to visit us in a couple of weeks and I wanted to talk to you about him before he gets here."

Harold was trying to line up the milk-soaked cornflakes so they made a yellow ring around the inside of the bowl. He maneuvered one from the bottom towards the rim.

"Are you still with me, darling?"

"Yeah, somone's coming to visit you said."

He was waiting for the punch line. The early phone call, the crying. It couldn't be just a simple visit. He concentrated on arranging the cornflakes.

"His name is Archie," she said very slowly and deliberately, "Archie Blatt and he comes from St. Louis."

The tone of her voice and the studied pace of the delivery made Harold feel as if he was being given a geography lesson. Aunt Enid obviously wanted him to know exactly where Archie Blatt came from.

She watched Harold closely as she spoke. He was messing around with his cereal, tensed, waiting for a blow to fall as if he knew already. How could be know?

"Now, Archie is a very old friend of mine, Harold and, well it's difficult to explain it, but... He sort of takes care of me... That is, not *takes care of me* actually, but we have this arrangement. He sort of pays for things, and... he comes to see me every once in a while...and..."

Harold glanced up from his bowl. He ducked his head when he met Enid's eyes coming at him from across the table. What was she trying to tell him?

"...he's sort of my boyfriend, if you know what I mean.

Although he's no boy, but..."

Harold thought he knew what she meant, although he didn't know what it meant for him.

"I told her that she was nothing better than a prostitute. Imagine, taking money like that."

"You shouldn't be so hard on her, Sylvia. It hasn't been easy for her."

"It hasn't been easy for us, Norman! That's no excuse for what she's doing there. Anyway, why are you defending her all of a sudden? You don't even like my sister. Wait a minute, do you like my sister?"

"That's not the point here. She likes the guy, right? If he wants to help her out..."

It was one of his parents' many conversations which he had heard but hadn't been able to put together with anything. He tried now but he didn't see how it fit with the phone call and the tears. There was something missing and that made him uneasy.

At least she had his attention. He had put down his spoon and looked at her. Maybe it wasn't going to be so difficult after all. She took a deep breath.

"When he comes I want you to be good friends with Archie, Harold. OK?"

It seemed important for Aunt Enid, and he didn't see what he had to lose.

"Sure, Aunt Enid. That's OK with me."

Meetings

He leaned his arms on the top rail of the rough wooden fence and watched the horses. Three of them stood together in the far corner of the corral. Only their tails moved, flicking away the flies. The smell was not nearly as bad as he had expected. In fact, he found he didn't mind the powerful rancid-sweet odor of horse shit and straw. That surprised him, for his only experience with horses had been a brief and unhappy one.

When he was little, about five or six, his mother had taken him to Pony Land near a big amusement park on Beverly near La Cienega. His legs too small to grip the animal's fat sides, he held on to the pommel and was bounced violently up and down as the pony trotted away from his mother and around the track. The ride seemed to last for hours. It was painful and he was so scared he wet his pants. They never went back. The only horses he saw after that were on television during the Rose Parade or in Westerns.

He loved Westerns. He cut school to go up to Hollywood to see the latest films like *Shane*, *Hondo*, *The Searchers*, *3:10 to Yuma* and tried not to miss anything on television. But it was the simple ritual formula that appealed to him, the good guys and the bad guys, not the horses. Real horses were for hayseeds, guys that talked slow and liked all that cornball, shitkicking music.

He was there at the stables, had braved the afternoon heat to escape from one of Aunt Enid's friends who had come to visit. Even horses were preferable.

"Harold, I want you to meet my very, *very* best friend, Charlene Briggs."

"Oh, it is so *nice* to see you, Harold. I've heard so *much* about you, dear, from your aunt," said Charlene, as if she was reciting from a book.

She stuck out her hand. Harold offered his. She took it in both of hers and didn't let go. Heavy rings dug into his knuckles. She was a tall, beefy woman who wore too much make-up. Her bouffant hairdo was stiff with lacquer.

"So, Harold, how are you liking our little ol' town?" she asked, giving him a warm smile and exchanging her accent for something much more Southern.

He couldn't get his hand back. She had a tight grip and seemed to be pulling him toward her. It was like being sucked into quicksand.

"Oh, um, ah... it's fine, I guess."

His ears felt hot, the palms of his hands sweaty. He knew he was blushing. Finally she let go. He almost fell over backwards. Both women laughed.

"Ain't he just the cutest little ol' thing?" said Charlene, winking at Harold and patting Enid on the thigh.

He mumbled something about getting a drink and rushed out of the room. When he reached the kitchen he kept going, the screen door banging loudly behind him. Aunt Enid called out after him, but he didn't listen. He put his head down and walked off towards the apparent shelter of the tamarisk trees at the end of the road. To his surprise, he had found the corral on the other side of the trees.

Now someone was walking towards him. Harold thought he looked familiar but he couldn't remember where he'd seen him.

"Hey, Harold, how they hangin'?"

Harold's memory of his sunstroke incident was not very clear, but from Aunt Enid's description he realized the boy must be the one who brought him home. Who else would know his name?

"Fine, yeah, thanks."

The boy stopped a few feet away and began to look Harold up and down as if he were a horse he might want to buy. The boy's stare made Harold uncomfortable.

"About the other day," said Harold, "... uh, thanks a lot for getting me home and all that."

"No sweat, partner. Couldn't let you lay out there and fry, could I? Wouldn't have been neighborly."

The boy seemed to have made up his mind. He laughed and punched Harold softly on the shoulder. Harold did not like being punched anywhere, however softly. Kids at school did it to each other all the time. Punching, slapping, wrestling, sometimes friendly sometimes not. On the whole, Harold found it easier to deal with the unfriendly, at least he didn't have to pretend to like it.

"No, I guess not," he said.

"You like horses?"

"Horses? Ah, I haven't had a lot to do with horses, if you know what I mean."

"City boy?"

Harold shrugged.

"Was that your mother out there the other day?"

"Nah, she's my aunt."

"Uh-huh... nice looking."

"I guess so."

Harold didn't want to think about Aunt Enid. He prayed the boy wouldn't go on about her. He looked across at the horses. They were moving slowly towards the two boys.

"By the by, the name's Earl, Earl Joe Earl. Father's named Earl as well. Earl Bob he is. Most folks call him Big Earl, though."

They shook hands. Firm and quick. Harold could live with that.

"Not a great time to come down for a visit. You know, the heat and all... Where you from anyways?"

"LA."

"You here for long?"

"Yeah, I'm afraid so."

Earl laughed and punched him again.

"Come on now, it ain't that bad! Where's your folks at?"

Reluctantly, Harold explained what had happened. The other boy was clearly impressed.

"Gee, I'm sorry. That is damn tough that is. Both of 'em going like that. Damn tough. My mom, you know, she's gone too."

Harold looked over at Earl.

"Died when I was baby. Can't rightly remember her at all."

Harold felt a stab of guilt for being able to remember his mother. He knew he was blushing. Shit!

They stood there not speaking. Earl kicked lightly at the dirt with the toe of his boot. After a few minutes the horses crossed the corral and came up to them. A big bay mare butted her head against

Earl's chest. He stroked her forehead, took a sugar cube out of his shirt pocket and put it on his palm. Rubbery lips enveloped the cube. The other two horses pushed towards him. He dug into his pocket again.

"These are the only ones we still got down here," he said. "Took the rest up to the high desert. A lot cooler there. Anyways, there ain't much call for riding this time of year. Too damn hot for the dudes, if you see what I mean."

Harold nodded. He could see exactly what Earl meant. The air was so dusty-hot he was finding it difficult to breathe. The glare coming off the white sand in the corral burned his eyes half shut. The summer desert was painful. Harold longed for the sheltered streets of the big city. Sure, it was hot there as well, but unless there was a Santa Anna blowing the heat was not so unremitting. Besides, he wasn't so exposed, so out in the open in LA He felt the sun searing the back of his neck. He pulled up his shirt collar.

"Well, partner, I gotta be getting back over there," Earl said pointing to a collection of low buildings on the other side of the corral. "Gotta shovel some shit outta the stalls and clean up the tack room or the old man'll kick my ass for sure. You wanna come over or something?"

It wasn't the best offer Harold had ever had, but when he thought of Charlene and Enid waiting for him at home, watching someone shovel shit didn't seem all that terrible. Anyway, it would get him inside. Inside had to be better.

The two boys walked towards the stables.

* * *

"He is a strange one, Enid. Ain't no doubt about that."

"Oh, he's alright really. I think he's just shy. Also I don't know whether he's got over the accident and all that. It's early days yet."

Charlene stuck her hand in her straw bag and took out a pack of L&M's. She offered the pack to Enid, who stared at it for a moment before reaching over and with the tips of her fingers slowly pulling out a cigarette. She held it up close to her face and studied it.

"For crying out loud, Charlene, you know I'm trying to quit."

"I know, honey. Sorry, you just give it me back. Come on."

Charlene reached for the cigarette. Enid smiled at her friend and put the cigarette in her mouth. Charlene shrugged, lit her own cigarette and held the match for Enid.

"Thanks."

They were quiet for a few moments, concentrating on drawing in the smoke.

"He don't half blush," laughed Charlene, the smoke dribbling from her nose.

"Yeah. It's having that red hair and light skin. That's what got him in all that trouble the other day when he fainted."

"You going to make out here with him, Enid? It ain't easy with a teenage kid, even at the best of times."

"Yeah, I know, but what can I do? I'm all he's got."

Charlene sucked on her cigarette and looked across at her friend.

"Shit, honey, you doing what's right. After all, the boy's kin, ain't he?"

Enid laughed. Sure he was family. He was *the* family.

"Jesus, Charlene, you still sound like such a darned Okie."

"What should I sound like?" she asked, stiffening. "I ain't ashamed like some others about being from Oklahoma. No, ma'am, I sure ain't ashamed of it."

"I suppose, but what's John say when you go on like that."

" 'Charlene, my dear'," she intoned in a deep, non-Oklahoma voice, " 'You must speak properly. It's not good for our position in the community or for business if my wife sounds like some ignorant pea picker.' "

Both women began to laugh.

" ' And I don't want our children talking like that either.' "

"How do you put up with that stuff?" asked Enid, wiping away the tears.

She stubbed her cigarette out in an El Mirador Hotel ashtray. She enjoyed stealing ashtrays.

"It ain't hard, honey. Not really anyway. I just ignore it mostly and get on. He ain't too bad. We get along pretty good. Speaking of which, you ain't said about Archie."

Enid told her about her phone call.

Charlene put her hand on Enid's knee and squeezed.

"I wouldn't worry yourself too much, honey. Archie's an alright fella. He'll understand you did the only thing you could do."

"I guess so," said Enid with no conviction.

She had never explained to Charlene the depth of Archie's hatred for kids.

"When's he getting here?"

"A week or so, I think. After he's finished with his business in Mexico."

"Yeah. You know, sometimes I wished John was away more. What you got here, this deal with Archie, well it ain't all bad."

"You got another cigarette, Charlene?"

They both lit up again. Enid stared out the window.

"Yeah," she said finally, "I'm maybe worrying too much about Archie."

"Sure, honey, sure you are. But, then he ain't met Harold yet, has he?"

Charlene laughed. Enid didn't.

"Come on, Enid honey," said Charlene, looking concerned. "I's only kidding with you."

Enid smiled and patted Charlene's hand.

"I know, it's just that he's about half a foot taller than Archie and..."

Charlene tried, but couldn't suppress a giggle.

"At least that," she said. "And, he's probably still growing."

"Charlene, don't!' cried Enid in desperation.

"Who knows, by the time Archie gets here..."

"Charlene, please!"

The stricken look on Enid's face shattered what little control Charlene had left. Within a few seconds both women were howling with laughter.

* * *

Harold grabbed the metal handles, tipped the wheelbarrow until it balanced on its wheel and pushed it along to the next stall. He maneuvered it through the door.

"That's good right there, Harold."

Earl threw a shovel full of horse shit into the wheelbarrow.

"You OK?"

"Yeah," replied Harold.

Unlike in the corral, in the narrow dark stalls the smell of horse shit and urine was acrid and concentrated. Just like Aunt Enid's perfume, it forced its way up Harold's nose. He was sweating and his shoulders had begun to ache. But, he didn't care. That surprised him for exercise did not feature prominently in Harold's life. He spent a lot of time avoiding it. He never went out for sports at school, cut gym class whenever he could. It wasn't just the exercise itself that bothered him.

"Come on Slim, move your fat ass! Four more laps. *Come* on!"

Harold gasped for breath, the sweat ran into his eyes, a painful stitch bit into his side as he staggered around the perimeter of the gymnasium. The rest of the class stood behind Mr. Peters and watched.

Years before, Mr. Peters had been a minor football star at one of the city high schools. He often talked about his triumphs to the boys, showed them yellowed newspaper clippings. He wore a baseball cap with a big **F** on the front, a silver-plated whistle on a string around his neck and he wanted everyone to call him "Coach." Harold was his favorite victim.

"You're carrying too much weight, Abelstein! You wanna wobble like that all your life? Come on! *Come* on!"

Harold hated PE, hated wearing white gym shorts, and most of all he hated Mr. Peters, whom he was always careful to call "Mr. Peters."

Earl chucked another shovel load into the wheelbarrow.

"Right, that's plenty. You take her out around the side there and you'll see a big pile. You just dump her onto that."

Harold nodded, hefted the wheelbarrow, turned it around and pushed it outside. As he walked between the row of stalls he tried to figure out why he, a kid who wasn't interested in physical exertion, horses, or heat, was struggling with a wheelbarrow full of horse shit. To get away from Aunt Enid and her friend? So he could hang out with Earl? But, Earl was a hick. He probably listened to country music, for Christ sake! Except for *not* being a golfer or a tennis player, which were two big pluses, Earl was all those other things which Harold had set himself to dislike about Palm Springs. But, he was also the first kid Harold had met there and as much as he hated to admit it, he found himself attracted to Earl. He seemed entirely at ease with himself and what he did. He could undoubtedly handle himself. Harold was sure he would know how to drive a truck and a tractor. He would know all about horses, why you needed different kinds of bits, how to clean a horse's hoof, the best rope to use, the right kind of spurs. Not that Harold had any interest in those stupid hick things, but he was ready to be impressed nonetheless. Most importantly, Earl seemed to accept Harold as Harold, not "Slim" or "Red" or "Fatty" or any of the other names he had been tagged with over the years. It was as if he was being invited to share in the mysteries of Earl's world with no questions asked.

"That's the last of 'em," said Earl putting the shovel over his shoulder. "You wanna drink?"

"Sure."

They walked back past the stalls to the stable office. Inside the door was a chest-type Coke machine. Earl lifted the lid. Bottles hung from their caps between rows of metal brackets. Earl slid a bottle to the front of the machine, put in a dime and pulled out a Coke. There was an opener nailed outside by the door. Earl stuck the head of the bottle in and pulled down. Dark bubbles foamed over the rim. He handed the bottle to Harold.

"That be OK, Harold?"

"Great, thanks."

On the table in the office was an old cream-colored Philco radio. Earl turned it on. Over the crackle of static boomed the deep voice of Tennessee Ernie Ford fog-horning out *Sixteen Tons*. There was nothing Harold could do about it. He sat down on the wooden steps next to Earl and drank his Coke.

It was late afternoon and although the sky was still painfully blue, the entire stables was in the shadow cast by the mountain. Earl tapped the heel of his boot on the bottom step in time to the music. He took off his hat and fanned himself.

"If you're going to be around here in the desert, Harold, you'd better latch on to one of these. Out here they ain't just for decoration."

Harold smiled. He might have hauled some horse shit, but he couldn't imagine himself wearing a cowboy hat. He was glad his LA friends couldn't see him covered in dirt, sitting outside on the steps with a cowboy and listening to Tennessee Ernie Ford.

* * *

"Harold! Where have you been? Just look at you! You're so filthy! And, darling, what is that *awful* smell?"

"Um, horses... Probably horses."

"Horses?"

"Uh-huh."

"Horses?" she repeated.

"I was over at the stables, you know down the end of the road there and I met this boy, the one who found me the other day and he sort of asked me to go there with him and..."

Enid was dumbfounded. Harold hadn't shown such enthusiasm, or talked so much all at one time since he came to Palm Springs.

"I was helping him a little with cleaning out the stalls and... Can I have a Coke or something?"

"Of course, darling."

She went into the kitchen, opened the refrigerator and took out a bottle. While she was opening it she called through to the living room.

"Tell me some more about what you did at the stables, Harold. Harold?"

Silence.

She came back into the living room and gave the opened Coke to Harold. Sprawled on one of the dining room chairs he looked absolutely exhausted, but for the first time Enid thought she detected a glimmer of something positive in her nephew's eyes.

"Thanks."

"Well, dear?"

"Yeah?"

"Tell me what happened at the stables?"

"Oh, yeah."

He tipped back the bottle.

"Well, this kid, Earl's his name, well, he took me around some, you know, and showed me the horses and stuff like that."

"I didn't know you were interested in horses, darling."

"Um, well, it's not that exactly, the horses I mean, you see, it's just... Well, you know it's kinda hard to explain it."

Harold couldn't put into words for Aunt Enid why he had liked being with Earl. He took another sip of Coke and tried to formulate an answer. Nothing came. He studied the picture of two big-eyed children which hung on the dining room wall opposite his chair.

She watched Harold struggling. No wonder he had trouble in school, she thought. Well, at least, he had found a friend. It breathed some life into him, although she was not altogether happy about the choice of Earl. It's true, he had been very polite to her, but was he really the kind of friend Harold needed? He was, if anything, more inarticulate than Harold and it was obvious he didn't come from a good family. She had envisaged Harold getting to know the children of her friends from the club. Well-spoken children who dressed nicely and wanted to go to college. But, what if he filled the house with kids like Earl, wearing cowboy boots, grunting at each other and smelling of horse manure? Christ Almighty! What would Archie have to say about that? After all, he was from St. Louis. She wondered if Harold's meeting Earl had been such a great idea.

"Aunt Enid, is it alright if I go to the drive-in tonight?"

"With your new friend?"

"Uh-huh."

"Does he have a car?"

"A pickup. He's got a pickup."

Enid's heart sank. A pickup truck! It figured he would have a pickup truck. She forced a smile.

"Of course you can go, darling. Just don't be back too late. OK?"

* * *

Harold had never been to a drive-in. He had never wanted to to go to a drive-in. He had had Hollywood Boulevard. Now he was reduced to going to a drive-in, just like kids in the Valley. He asked what was on, but Earl didn't know.

"Well," offered Harold, "shouldn't we check or something? I mean, maybe there's something better on in town."

Earl laughed and punched Harold on the shoulder. Harold

supposed he was going to have to get used to being punched on the shoulder.

"Shit, Harold, it's Friday night! We always go out to the Sun-Air on a Friday night."

"Yeah, OK, but, what if you don't want to see the movie or if you've seen it already?"

"It don't really matter much. You'll see."

Harold was puzzled. How could it not matter? Why else would you want to go the movies? He did often wander up to Hollywood without knowing what he was going to see. That wasn't a problem because there were so many movie theaters he could always find something good. A drive-in in the middle of the desert was an entirely different proposition.

It was about 8:00 when Harold heard the horn of Earl's pickup.

Aunt Enid was sitting in the living room painting her fingernails. She had just come out of the shower and was wearing a white terry cloth robe, her hair wrapped in a towel. As he moved towards the front door she put down the bottle of polish and stood up carefully holding her wet nails out in front of her.

"Now remember, darling, not too late. If I'm not home when you get back I'll leave the key under the mat out by the kitchen."

She followed him to the door. The belt of her robe had come loose, and the two bits of cloth were beginning to part. Aunt Enid didn't notice. Harold did. He saw the brown mound of a breast starting to emerge. The horn sounded again outside. He backed towards the front door.

"Have a nice time, Harold."

She took another step. The robe opened further. He could now see both of her breasts almost to the nipples and the fleshy inside of one thigh. He looked up at his aunt and forced a smile.

"Uh, yeah , thanks, Aunt Enid, I will."

He fumbled behind him for the doorknob, opened the door just enough to let himself out. He didn't want Earl to see Aunt Enid. He tried to slide out of the doorway sideways. He was too wide for such a delicate maneuver.

"What's the matter, Harold? Can't you see, darling?"

Aunt Enid reached for the light switch. The bright light over the door came on, blinding Harold momentarily. As Enid moved, the robe flapped open and her breasts and a triangle of dark pubic hair flashed glaringly at Harold. He let out a soft mewing sound and stepped backwards, hurriedly trying to close the door at the same time. It didn't work. The heel of his foot hit the doormat and he toppled over, crashing flat on his back onto the flagstone path, exposing a floodlit Aunt Enid to Earl and some other boys waiting in the pickup.

"Way to go!" a voice shouted.

Someone else gave a loud wolf whistle.

From the ground Harold looked up and saw his aunt, her robe now firmly gathered together, moving down the path towards him.

"Harold? Are you alright, dear?"

"Fine," he whispered pleadingly. "Fine."

She bent to help him. He scrambled to his feet and ran for the pickup. He didn't look back.

Mourning After

She sat in the living room staring out into the back yard. Reflecting off the white gravel and the pool, the morning sun sliced into her eyes. She closed them slowly. It didn't help, the throbbing ache in her head remained. Her stomach felt hollow and queasy. She was hungry but couldn't face the thought of eating.

Next to her on the coffee table were dirty glasses, two empty bottles of wine and a full ashtray, the tips of the crushed butts ringed with red lipstick. The room reeked of stale smoke. There was a half-empty pack of cigarettes on the floor. Charlene's L&M's. Her friend hadn't left until well after two in the morning.

Enid got up shakily and pulled the belt of her robe tight around her waist. She pushed open the sliding door and stepped outside. The smooth concrete was warm under her feet. She took a deep breath. The dry air made her cough. She grabbed a canvas-backed chair, dragged it into the shade of a palm tree by the pool and sat down heavily. From one of her pockets she pulled out a large pair of sunglasses. The world looked marginally better after she put them on although she still felt awful.

Enid had never been much of a drinker. That was a handicap, for drinking was the essence of social life in Palm Springs. The night before she had gone out to dinner with Charlene. Charlene didn't find drinking a problem.

"Come on honey, cheer up, get another drink into you. You look like the ol' well's run dry."

"Charlene, will you can that down-home stuff, please."

Charlene looked hurt. She signaled to the waiter.

"This time, Bobby, dry, dry. OK? And I'd like two of them little ol' olives."

The waiter nodded, folded the small round tray under his arm and walked over to the bar. Charlene watched his behind as he crossed the room.

"He's sorta cute, huh?"

"Come on, Charlene! He's a kid, for Christ's sake."

"I dunno," she said speculatively, "he's gotta be over twenty-one. Yeah, at least over twenty-one."

"And you gotta be out of your tiny mind."

Enid sipped her drink and while Charlene bent down to get something from her purse she turned and had a quick look at the waiter. He was leaning with his elbows on the bar talking to the bartender. They were both laughing. The waiter had shiny dark hair and a trim body. Enid compared him to Archie. She tried to picture the young waiter naked in her bed. She couldn't decide if it was an interesting picture or not. Her daydream was interrupted by Charlene's voice.

"So?" cackled Charlene. "You are interested after all."

Enid blushed.

"Not really," she replied, trying to recover, "just looking, just thinking."

Charlene leaned across the table. She lowered her voice.

"Yeah, Enid honey, I know, just looking, just thinking. I mean like thinking about doing it with a really young guy like that? I mean, you know, like how it used to be? All them firm muscles, that excitement, that energy, not to mention them being able to keep their little dingus up for more than a couple-a-three minutes."

Enid smiled. Charlene was always so direct about things. It was refreshing. The women she was friendly with at the club were much more circumspect in conversation. They did share intimacies, complained a lot about their husbands, most of whom only came down to see them on weekends, but if they were having affairs they were careful not to mention them. Palm Springs was a very small town.

"You've got sex on the brain, Charlene Briggs."

"And why not? Shee-it, honey ol' John he gets himself interested maybe once a week, if that. And when he does it don't last long. Wham, bam and then there ain't no 'Thank you ma'am' neither. Rolls off and goes to sleep, snoring, his belly going up and down like a hound dog in a heat wave. Hell's fire, we're — you and me that is..." Charlene's voice took on a more precise tone, "we're at the peak of our sexual power just about now. You knew that, didn't you?"

Enid choked on her drink. It was all she could do not to spit it up.

"Where'd you get that from?" she finally managed to say.

"In some book or other I was looking at, can't remember what it was called. Guy's name's Have-a something-or-other. In there it says that we hit the top of our sex lives about thirty-five or forty, whereas for men it's all down hill after eighteen. Poor bastards. Shee-it, honey, eighteeen! Can you believe that? I mean to say, that goes to explaining a lot of things, don't it?"

She sat back and laughed. The waiter brought her two-olive martini, put a paper coaster on the table and set the glass down carefully. Charlene gave him a warm smile.

"Thanks a load, honey. You ready for another now, Enid?"

She nodded and the waiter moved off again. This time both women watched his progress back to the bar.

Enid shook her head ruefully. She took one of Charlene's cigarettes and lit it. Tomorrow she would stop smoking. Definitely tomorrow. She looked across the table at her friend.

"Charlene, what the hell am I going to do about Archie?"

Charlene wasn't paying attention, her eyes still lingered on the waiter.

"Charlene!"

"Yeah. What?"

"Archie. What am I going to do?"

Charlene gave a last look at the waiter and then turned to face Enid.

"I really don't know. It's a tough one, no getting round it... Hey listen, Enid honey, how's about this. When Archie comes you can send Harold over to our place. He can stay in the spare room. I reckon Big John won't mind."

"What about Joan and John, Jr.?"

"You don't wanna worry about them two, they're still away to camp. God, I don't know what I'd do without that summer camp."

"Gee, Charlene, that's real nice of you to offer and all, but I... Ah, I don't know."

"No trouble, honey and if you do that Archie don't have to know nothing. He'll be here, what, a week, ten days? That ain't long. Whadda you think?"

It was very tempting. It would make everything much easier for her. She saw the pain on Archie's face as he told her about his daughters. Then she saw Harold's face at the funeral, saw him looking around his new room, saw his records all neatly arranged in boxes, saw him watching television, saw him lying in a red-faced heap on the ground in front of the house. She shook her head.

"But, I can't do it, Charlene. It wouldn't be right."

"I'm telling you, honey, it would be OK. There is..."

"I know that, but it's Harold. I can't do it to Harold. Poor kid. Shunting him around like that when he's just barely settled. No, I appreciate it, Charlene, but I just can't."

Enid felt guilty for even having thought about it. Charlene shrugged and picked up her drink.

"Maybe you're right on that, honey. Maybe. But then you're just going to have to tell Archie straight out when he gets here."

"Yeah," said Enid, resigned to her fate. "I know that. I suppose I've known that all along."

Neither of them spoke for a few minutes.

"This damn place, it's so dead!" exclaimed Charlene, blowing out a jet of smoke and sweeping her arm around to take in the empty restaurant.

"It's the same everywhere," Enid said. "You know that."

"Yeah, of course I know that. Still and all, it don't make it any easier or any less dead."

Between mid-July and September the population of the town dropped by three-quarters to only about 12,000. The Chi Chi, the town's only nightclub, didn't book any class acts, only a pick-up band for the few people who wanted to dance. The piano bar in the Garden Room at the Biltmore was definitely *not* the spot, and although the Palm House had decided for the first time to hire a singing trio for the summer, they had been taken off after a couple of weeks. No one came because the feeling was that if you had to play Palm Springs in the summer you weren't worth going to see. Many of the big hotels, where in the season you could find a singer or a small dance band, were shut, as were most of the good restaurants. Even the Racquet Club, which boasted New Year's Eve every night, was closed.

The only people who stayed in Palm Springs during the summer were those who for one reason or another couldn't afford to escape to somewhere cooler. The Agua Caliente Indians, to whom the government had so thoughtfully given about half of their own land, they couldn't escape. Neither could the working people who kept the place going: guys that cleaned the pools, policemen, firemen, gas station attendants, plumbers, gardeners, real estate agents — like Charlene's husband — check-out clerks at Mayfair, Safeway and at Thrifty Drugs, carpenters, doctors, and mailmen. None of them could get out. Neither could Enid. Archie's wallet didn't stretch to two houses. Summer in the desert was really tough for her, and it didn't make it any better knowing her misery was shared.

Enid moved the chair closer to the pool and stuck her feet into the water. The coolness soothed her, seemed to travel upwards clearing her head, easing the pain behind her eyes. She was thinking about having a quick swim when she heard the side gate open. A few moments later a young man wearing nothing but a pair of cut-off Levis and tennis shoes appeared carrying a pool skimmer and a large bottle of chlorine.

"Hi, Mrs. Carlson. How you doing today?"

"Fine, Manny. Just fine. How are you?"

"Not bad really, that is considering..."

He sat down on the diving board. Enid got up hurriedly and started for the house. She wasn't in any condition for one of Manny's endless, rambling conversations. They were always more endless, more rambling in the summer when he rarely found anyone to talk to out by the swimming pools. She stopped at the door and turned around.

"Manny darling, don't put the chlorine in just now. I want to have a swim soon. I'll put it in myself later. OK?"

"Sure thing, Mrs. Carlson. That's no trouble at all. I'll just leave it here, where..."

Enid went inside and slid the door closed firmly behind her.

* * *

SUN-AIR DRIVE-IN
HORROR DOUBLE BILL
THE INCREDIBLE SHRINKING MAN
THE CREATURE FROM THE BLACK LAGOON
Complete Show from Sundown

The sign was the only illumination on the long stretch of darkness which ran beside Highway 111 just outside Cathedral City, a small town a few miles from Palm Springs. Behind the circle of light the big screen, like a giant curved wall, rose straight up over a hundred feet from the desert floor. Above it was the sky, white with stars. A clapboard fence curved away from either side of the screen and out into the desert. Earl turned the pickup off onto the dirt road and stopped abruptly at the side of a small wooden hut. The cloud of following dust washed over Harold and the other two boys sitting in the the back of the truck. From the ticket window a middle-aged woman in a sleeveless flower-print dress stared out at them. Her fleshy arms were pock-mark white. She leaned forward, squinting through her glasses, carefully counting the number of boys in the truck.

"How many?" she asked suspiciously.

"Just what you see here, ma'am," replied Earl, nodding towards the back of the truck.

Hands pressed hard down on the table, she stood up to get a better look, to make sure no one was lying down out of sight, trying to sneak in without paying. Having satisfied herself, she let her body collapse back into the chair and counted out six tickets. Her lips moved silently over each number.

"That'll be six dollars."

Earl handed her the money and took the tickets.

"Thank you kindly," he said, touching the brim of his hat.

"Y'all behave yourselves now!" she called after them.

Harold and his companions held on as Earl gunned the truck into the drive-in.

One of the movies had already started. Up on the screen a man and a woman were talking to each other on the deck of a boat. Harold had seen this one before. He reckoned it had taken two or three years for *The Creature from the Black Lagoon* to make the

Sun-Air Drive-In. He sighed, closed his eyes and tried to picture Hollywood Boulevard at night: the brightly-lit marquees, the record stores, the crowds, the noise, the excitement. His friends would probably be there now, walking around trying to decide which movie to go see. And, here he was in the middle of nowhere bouncing around with a couple of hicks in the back of a pickup truck. At least he hadn't been able to hear the country music from Earl's radio on the drive out. He was thankful for that.

He opened his eyes. The place was full of the dark shapes of cars all on slight rakes, their noses pointing up towards the screen. They looked expectant, reverential. Earl turned off his headlights and drove slowly to the very back of the lot. He parked with the cab facing away from the screen.

"You OK, Harold?" asked Earl, swinging up into the back of the truck.

"Uh-huh, fine."

"You met Jingles and Tommy," said Earl. "That there's Tody, Tommy's little brother, and this one here is Garf."

"How the fuck ya doing, Big Red?" said Garf, clambering over the tailgate.

He was a little guy with bandy legs. When he got closer and smiled, Harold saw he had buck teeth and fierce, slightly crossed eyes. Like all the others he wore boots and a cowboy hat.

Garf had a cocky bantam swagger and squeezed extra hard when he shook hands. Harold recognized him as the kind who invariably gave him a bad time. Taller and heavier than most kids his own age, Harold was the target for every little guy with a chip on his shoulder. There seemed to be a never-ending supply of them. Even his music and the implicit protection of the Negro kids couldn't save him from their attention.

"Come on, Big Man. You wanna get into it? Huh? What's a matter, you pussy or what?"

Harold never made eye contact. That would have been fatal. Instead he would smile to himself and walk away. Sometimes they would grab his arm or push him, trying to provoke a response. Harold didn't respond. He didn't know the first thing about fighting and had no desire to learn. It seemed utterly pointless and inescapably painful.

"Sure, yeah, look at him go. Chicky, chicky... Big Man!"

Harold found he could live with that. After a while they got bored and left him alone.

But Garf seemed friendly enough. It was the other kid, Tody, who was touchy. He never looked up, never acknowledged Harold, just grunted angrily and wandered off into the dark.

"Don't pay him no never mind," said Earl. "His old lady dumped him and he's pissed is all."

"I hope to hell, he don't go and find her here with that there Carpenter guy," said Tommy anxiously.

Tommy was a skinny kid. His ears stuck out.

"Shit, Tommy, you ain't scared of that dumb fuck? Let him find Carpenter," snorted Garf, puffing up. "Shit man, we'll kick us some ass for sure!"

He slammed his boot into the side of the truck. It gave a hollow ring.

"Fuck yes we will!" Garf spat.

"You wanna go easy on the truck, Tiger?" cautioned Earl.

"You guys wanna watch this movie or what?" asked Jingles, reaching over and grabbing the speaker from the pole.

Somewhere from the mass of dark cars in front of them came the sound of breaking glass. A girl screamed. No one took any notice, except Harold. He wanted to ask about it but felt he shouldn't. If it was important someone would tell him.

"Yeah, OK," answered Earl. "You calm yourself now, Garf, little buddy. We don't want no bother with that crowd tonight. Who's got the brew?"

"You say," shot back Garf.

"That's right, Peanut, I say," Earl said with friendly menace.

Harold felt the tension. He didn't like it. At Fairfax High he had developed a highly sensitive nose for trouble and worked on his moves to avoid it. He made sure he posed no threat to anyone, that he didn't hang out with guys who got into fights. And, there was the music. His fierce and specialized knowledge was like a magic shield setting him apart and protecting him. But out here in the desert night no one knew him or cared about the invaluable, detailed rhythm-and-blues lore that he carried around in his head. And he didn't know who was who or exactly what was going on.

Newborn and helpless in a desert drive-in movie. A big fat kid. A big soft target.

He stared out into the darkness. A car door slammed. Someone shouted. Shadows danced among the parked cars. Up on the screen the girl was just about to go for a swim in the lagoon. He couldn't understand why she wanted do that. He wouldn't have done it. Harold hoped that Tody didn't find Carpenter. Five minutes ago he hadn't heard of either of them. Now he was involved. He wished he had stayed home.

Tommy picked up a gunny sack, took out a six-pack of beer and began handing them around.

"You like Country Club?" Jingles asked Harold.

Harold knew nothing about alcohol. He had tried the occasional drink at friends' houses when their parents were out, but he didn't particularly like the taste. He was told he would have to get used to it, that it was an acquired taste, like drinking black coffee. It didn't make any sense to him that someone should want to acquire a taste for something he didn't like. So, he had never bothered.

He took the can from Jingles. It was a little more than half the size of an ordinary beer can.

"Guess so, sure, thanks," Harold lied. "Where'd you get it at?"

"My brother's got an I.D. He always buys for us. You got some money to chip in?"

"Yeah, sorry, sure I do. How much?"

"A couple of bucks'll be alright."

It seemed a lot of money for a can of beer, especially such a small can, but Harold decided not to say anything. He took out his wallet and gave Jingles two dollars.

"Anyone got a fucking church key?" said Garf.

"Here," said Earl. "Now shut up, willya?"

Harold leaned back against the cab of the truck and sipped his beer. It was awful. Thick and lukewarm. On the screen the Creature was climbing onto the boat. Harold took another sip. It still tasted awful.

"Lizard fuck!" shouted Garf.

Earl leaned over and knocked off the smaller boy's hat. It sailed over the side of the truck.

"Ah, shit, Earl! Come on," Garf whined.

He got out to retrieve his hat.

The boys drank steadily. Harold winced as each empty can clanged loudly against the concrete. He had to force himself to finish his.

Next to him, Jingles was crushing an empty can in his big hand. He was short and burley, had a tattoo of a rose on his left upper arm and a long scar running down the side of his neck. Here was just the kind of kid Harold had successfully avoided at high school.

Jingles caught Harold looking. Harold tried to avert his eyes, but the other boy didn't seem to mind the stare.

"Fight with some greasers," he explained, fingering the scar. "Bastard had a straight razor. Broke his fucking arm and his fucking jaw."

"Come on, son," he said, handing Harold an open can. "You got another four coming."

Another four, thought Harold despairingly. He already felt sick to his stomach from the first can which was sloshing around on top of Aunt Enid's somewhat suspect corned beef hash.

Just then Tommy announced he was going to get some popcorn.

"I'll go with you," said Harold, seeing his chance to escape from Jingles and the four unfinished cans of beer. Maybe the others would drink them before he got back.

"I gotta take a leak," explained Harold, putting down the can.

"Don't you go and piss in the popcorn now, Red," Garf called helpfully.

The two boys walked between the parked cars towards a low building in the center of the drive-in. The movie soundtrack ebbed and flowed as they passed by the open windows.

"Hey, man," laughed Tommy, "your aunt, she sure got a nice pair of knockers on her."

Not him too, thought Harold. He didn't answer, pleased that it was dark. He looked up at the screen. They had captured the Creature. It always made him sad when that happened. Fucking thing out there swimming around in the middle of a pond minding its own business.

"No offense, OK?" said Tommy, uneasy at Harold's silence.

"Sure," answered Harold after a moment, "no offense."

Outside the building they saw Tody. He paced back and forth in front of the door, head down, muttering to himself.

"Hey, Little Brother," called Tommy, "What's the matter, huh?"

The other boy looked up. His heavy shoulders, well-muscled arms and scowling face made him look older than his nervously-scrawny big brother.

"Nothing," he replied sullenly.

"You find Kathy, or what?"

Tody stopped pacing. He banged his fist into his open hand.

"Shit no, I didn't. I saw Robertson over there."

He pointed towards the front of the drive-in.

"Said Carpenter and them others ain't here tonight. At the bowling alley or something. Shit!"

Harold felt the knot of fear in his stomach loosen slightly. No Carpenter, no troubles. Maybe he would make it through the night after all.

"You wanna get something to eat or what?" asked Tommy.

Tody didn't answer. He walked off into the darkness.

"That there is one pissed-off dude," said Tommy. "Glad he didn't come across old Carpenter though. Guy's a fucking animal. Football player. Don't know what I would have told Mom if he got himself beat up. She's always saying how I've got to look after my little brother. But you just look at the idiot, willya. How do you reckon I'm supposed to look after him?"

Harold smiled to himself. He was glad he wasn't the only one who wanted to stay out of trouble.

They pushed open the door to the refreshment stand. Harold squinted against the fluorescent glare. On each end of a long counter electric fans blew the hot air back and forth. The whole place smelled of popcorn, rancid butter and cigarette smoke. The cracked cement floor was stained, covered in cigarette butts and candy wrappers. There were only a few customers milling around. Doris Day's voice squeaked out at them from a loudspeaker high in one corner.

"Now's the time to come, before the rush," said Tommy. "Wadda you want?"

Harold looked up at the loudspeaker. First Pat Boone, he thought, and now Doris Day. He belched, tasting the Country Club and a not-so-gentle hint of corned beef hash.

"Some popcorn's alright," answered Harold.

"Right. Hey Wayne," Tommy shouted to the tall skinny boy behind the counter. "Give us a couple a boxes of popcorn, willya? And a Three Musketeers, OK?"

"Right," the boy replied without a smile, adjusting the small paper hat on his head.

"Wayne here's a real friendly cuss, ain't you Wayne?"

The boy stared dull-eyed at Tommy. Slowly he scooped popcorn into the boxes. He glanced up. Across the room the manager, wearing a short-sleeved white shirt and a string tie, was watching him intently. The manager rocked slightly on the balls of his feet, a tight smile on his face.

"You always was a dumb-fuck cowboy," Wayne whispered harshly, not looking at Tommy or Harold.

"You just keep on trucking now, shit-for-brains," Tommy laughed, taking the candy bar and the popcorn.

He handed a box to Harold. There was a loud screech from the loudspeaker. Someone had dropped the needle onto a new record. The manager looked up at the loudspeaker. He shook his head with resignation. The music began again. Harold sighed.

It wasn't R & B, but given how things were the Del Vikings were a definite improvement over Doris Day.

"Hi there," someone behind him said.

Startled, Harold turned. A small blond girl stood next to him.

"Remember me?" she said, pouting slightly.

Harold didn't. He could feel a blush starting up his neck.

"Uh, no... Sorry, can't say that I do."

"The drugstore... Come on, you know. We still got your old straw hat in the back somewheres."

She laughed, mouth open wide. Then he remembered — the steel-toothed Pat Boone fan.

"Oh, yeah. Hi."

"How you doing?" she asked.

"OK. Just fine, you know, just fine, uh-huh," he said, nodding and smiling.

Tommy stood next to Harold, staring uneasily at the girl. He shifted about for a few minutes, looked over his shoulder and then tugged on Harold's shirt.

"Come on, Harold, let's go, huh," he said impatiently.

"Sure," replied Harold, eyeing the girl as if she were a coiled snake.

Holding his box of popcorn against his chest, he began slowly to back towards the door. He had heard that when you came across a rattler in the desert you didn't want to make any sudden movement. The girl followed him, smiling. He bumped into something. A few pieces of popcorn sprayed out of the box and fell onto the floor.

"Why don't you watch where you're going, Fatman!"

The hair on the back of Harold's neck stood up. He took a step forward and swung around slowly. A short thickset boy stared up at him. Why, thought Harold, why do they always find me? And, why do they always look like they're auditioning for a part in *The Blackboard Jungle*? This one wore a black leather jacket, his greasy hair combed back in a ducktail and forward in an elaborate waterfall. His body seemed to be in constant motion, shoulders swinging, fingers snapping. Behind him were two other boys, also wearing leather jackets. They watched eagerly.

Harold knew he was going to fart. He always did when he was about to take a pounding. He squeezed the cheeks of his ass together as tightly as he could and prayed.

"Uh... I'm sorry," said Harold, looking down at the floor.

"Sorry? Sorry? Wadda you mean, sorry? And, you're talking to my girl. What you think you're doing, huh?"

"Sorry," repeated Harold, the pitch of his voice rising, his panic rising and his bowls rumbling

"Come on Johnny," said the girl. "Leave him alone. He weren't doing nothing. And like I told you before, I ain't your girl neither!"

The boy ignored her. He took a step closer to Harold, bent down and picked up a piece of popcorn from the floor. He studied it carefully. It was covered in dirt. He rolled it back and forth between his thumb and forefinger, caressing it. Harold couldn't take his eyes from the piece of popcorn.

"Well, look what we got us here. The Fatman's spilled some of his popcorn. Can't have that, can we, Fatman?"

The boy reached up and carefully put the filthy piece on the top of the popcorn in Harold's box.

Out of the corner of his eye Harold saw Tommy edging towards the door. He was on his own. He wished he wasn't holding a box of popcorn. It made him feel more vulnerable. With a loud report, as if someone had popped a blown-up paper bag, a fart sneaked through his defenses. Luckily the fearsome noise of his fear seemed to have got lost in between the sound of the music and the noise of the fans.

"Just so as you don't spill no more popcorn," said the boy.

He put his hand on the top of the box and pushed hard. The bottom split open and popcorn rained down on Harold's shoes. He kept hold of the empty box. He couldn't think what else to do with it.

"OK, boys. OK. Outside. We don't want any trouble in here."

It was the manager. He put himself between the two boys.

"Hey, man, I'm just trying to help this here kid with his popcorn," said the boy, flashing an innocent grin.

"If you're not out of here in ten seconds flat," the manager said, "I'll call the cops. Now, out! All of you, out!"

The three leatherjackets laughed loudly and sauntered out the door.

Harold stood his ground. The last thing he wanted to do was to go outside. They would be waiting for him.

"You too, son. Out!"

"But... I wasn't doing nothing," pleaded Harold. "It was..."

He farted again. This time with such monumental power and venom that neither music nor electric fans could disguise it. The manager looked at him in disgust. Wayne, the kid behind the counter, laughed out loud.

"Out!" the manager repeated, his face reddening and his quivering finger pointing straight towards the door.

Harold looked around for some support, but the girl had gone, Tommy had gone and the few other people in the room were busy not paying attention. Only Wayne was watching, and he had a self-satisfied smirk on his face.

Reluctantly, Harold walked towards the exit. Sweat ran down his sides, his mouth was dry and he had given up trying to control his wind. He closed his eyes and pushed the door open, tensing for the blow. Nothing happened. Very cautiously he opened his eyes. There was no one there. He held his breath, listening, but all he could hear was the muffled sound of the movie soundtrack coming from the parked cars. The film was almost over. The Creature had escaped and was swimming away, wounded but still alive, back to the deep safety of the Black Lagoon.

* * *

He was woken by the sound of the sliding door in the living room banging closed. The dull noise thumped inside his head, then it tried to get out again by pushing painfully against the back of his eyes. He sat up. The outside brightness cut at him through the uncurtained window. He was still wearing all his clothes, even his shoes. He gazed down at his feet. No socks. He couldn't understand why he was wearing shoes but no socks. He belched, his mouth filling with the taste of bile. Struggling to his feet he blundered into the hallway.

"Good morning, Harold darling. Had a..."

Enid stopped, taking in the bloodshot eyes and the patches of encrusted vomit on his shirt, on his trousers, on his shoes. She thought she detected strings of red meat caught in the swirling yellow stains.

"Why Harold," Aunt Enid cried in alarm, "have you been sick, dear?"

In reply, Harold's stomach heaved. A low gurgling sound moved up his throat, his cheeks puffed out and he ran for the bathroom. He just made it. Slamming the door behind him, he fell on his knees, embraced the sides of the toilet and retched. A thin trickle of liquid dripped from his mouth into the bowl. His stomach and throat contracted in unison again and again. His mouth opened wide but nothing came out. He knew he was dying. The process wasn't helped by the insistent voice on the other side of the door.

"Harold? What's the matter, darling? Harold?"

Enid stood outside the bathroom. She rattled the knob. The door was locked.

"Please, darling, open the door. Let me see what's wrong. Harold? Harold, please!"

Enid was frightened. She hadn't thought about the possibility of Harold getting sick. Problems about school, about his lack of friends, about grief over his parents' death, but not illness. He was so big and solid, so young. She had never had to think about anybody but herself and she had always been so healthy. Sickness, like children, was for other people. Even her mother had had the decency not to linger. A neighbor called her at work and by the time she got home her mother was already dead. A heart attack the doctor said. Quick and painless.

Maybe it was the corned beef? She hadn't eaten any. It could have been the corned beef. How serious was food poisoning? On the other side of the door the toilet was flushed. She listened intently. It was very quiet in the bathroom. Had he passed out?

"Please, Harold. I'm worried. Come on, darling, open the door."

She tried the handle once more.

Harold sat on the floor with his back against the cool porcelain of the bathtub. He was sweating heavily, panting, trying to ignore his aunt and trying to remember what had happened the night before.

"OK, OK. At least tell me you're alright, that you haven't hurt yourself or anything... Harold?"

"Yeah, alright," came the mumbled reply. "Alright."

Harold had been outside the refreshment stand at the drive-in only a few moments when Earl arrived with the other boys. They'd been running.

"You alright, Harold?" asked Earl.

"Yeah, thanks, I'm OK."

"Where are they at?" Garf asked, looking around for the opposition, tapping a tire iron against his leg.

"Dunno," said Harold, shrugging his big shoulders. "Gone."

"Oh shit! Fucking, cunt-licking shit!" fumed Garf.

He smacked the tire iron on the ground.

"Cool down, boy," cautioned Earl, "you'll do yourself an injury."

"They didn't wanna fuck with Harold is all," said Tommy proudly.

Back at the pickup they treated Harold like a hero. It seemed that Tommy had embellished the story of the confrontation somewhat. In his version Harold had been trying to pick up this neat chick when he was jumped by five big guys in leather jackets. Harold's protestations were brushed aside.

"Come on, man," said Jingles, laying a heavy hand on his arm, "have a drink. You deserve it."

Harold had a drink.

After a few more cans of Country Club, Jingles became more loquacious. He patted Harold's hand affectionately.

"You know something, Harold. You ain't like them other Jews at school. No, not like 'em at all. Why's that?"

He put his face close to Harold's and grinned. His breath smelled sickly green. His teeth were small and yellow; one of the front ones was missing. Harold tried to pull away.

"What?" replied Harold, increasingly befuddled by the booze.

He was trying to make some sense out of the movie. The little guy was living in a doll's house and a giant cat was trying to get at him. Harold giggled.

"You know, Jews, Jews. Jews, you know? Huh? Like all those guys always being so smart in class and that. Christ!" he said punching Harold softly on the chin, "you don't even look like a goddamned Jew."

Through the alcohol haze Harold felt a tingle of fear. Jews? Why was the Tattoo talking about Jews? At Fairfax everyone was Jewish, except, of course, the Negro kids. He hadn't really thought about not being surrounded by Jews or about being Jewish. His parents were what he thought of as Gefilte-Fish Jews. They ate some of the food — Jewish, not kosher — and had a few words of Yiddish and on account of Israel they hated the Arabs. The Abelsteins' Jewish didn't make it as far as a Yorhzeit candle or a synagogue. Harold hadn't even had a bar mitzvah. So for him what was a Jew? Did it matter?

"Leave him alone," said Earl.

"I ain't doing nothing," retorted Jingles with drunken indignity.

"It's OK," said Harold.

"Sure," Jingles said, draping a thick arm on Harold's shoulder. "We're good buddies. Ain't that right, Harold?"

He gave Harold a hard squeeze.

"Right," muttered Harold. "Buddies. Good buddies. Jew buddies."

Jingles handed him another can of Country Club. He drank. It was starting to taste better or at least not taste as bad. After that, his memory faded out almost completely. He couldn't remember how he had got home. He wondered what had happened to the little guy in the movie. He wondered what had happened to his socks.

"Should I call the doctor, Harold?"

Aunt Enid. How would he explain this to her? Once his father had come home drunk very late at night. Harold had been woken by his mother's shouting.

"...just like my father!"

Harold listened, holding his breath. His mother rarely mentioned her father, except when she was very angry.

"Sylvia, come on," his father begged. "I just had a couple of..."

"In the bathroom! You wanna come home like that, you can sleep in the bathroom!"

A door slammed, then silence. Harold lay awake for a long time that night.

"Harold? Was it the corned beef, Harold?"

"What? Ah, dunno ... I'm going to have a shower now."

"OK, darling, but be careful."

Enid tightened the belt of her robe. She listened until she heard the water running and then went into the kitchen and made a pot of fresh coffee. The rich smell helped clear her head.

Harold and Enid and Abe

Maybe It Wasn't Necessary...

When he had finally emerged from the bathroom Harold looked so miserable, so serious, that Enid had felt a wave of real affection for him, affection heightened by her relief that his terminal illness was only a bad hangover. She decided maybe he wasn't such a hopeless case after all. He did have sort of a nice face. Bright blue eyes and a strong nose. If he smiled more his mouth would be OK too. It was generous and warm. In fact, if he lost a few pounds he could be quite handsome really. She half closed her eyes and tried to transform Harold. She couldn't quite do it.

It bothered her that these intense feelings for her nephew came only when he was in distress. She thought perhaps that was normal, but she didn't really know.

Later, in the early evening, she stood in the doorway to the kitchen, the wave of morning affection receding as she watched the light from the TV flicker across Harold's pale face.

"I'll be back about 11:00, Harold."

"Uh-huh."

Ernie Bilko was setting up yet another elaborate scheme to make money. It involved golf and Colonel Hall and Palm Springs. A sure disaster. Besides it was a rerun. He knew how it ended. Harold leaned back, making himself more comfortable on the couch.

"Did you hear me, Harold?"

He answered without taking his eyes from the screen.

"Yeah. Uh-huh. OK."

"Are you feeling alright now, darling?"

"Fine. Sure, I'm fine. Thanks."

When he told her what had happened at the drive-in, at least some of the scenes he remembered, she had laughed and hugged him. Her reaction surprised Harold. He was expecting a lot of yelling, followed by a cautionary sermon. He was beginning to understand that, unlike his mother, Aunt Enid was not one for yelling or for cautionary sermons. That made him think about his mother. Suddenly he missed her terribly and he had gone into his room and wept, less for her than for himself. Loss, abandonment, self-pity, guilt. The emotions all ran into each other and then joined forces with the hangover. He didn't try to figure it out. Instead he had played his records. Comfortingly, they were always exactly the same — tunes, lyrics, singers, the color of the labels.

He had spent the day being pampered by Aunt Enid. Alka-Seltzer followed by dry toast and tomato juice. He was grateful for her attention, but after a while, when he started to feel better, her concern began to crowd him once again and he retreated as best he could.

Enid checked her hair in the mirror by the front door. She put her lips together and rolled them back and forth against one another to even out her lipstick. She grabbed her purse and opened the door. Harold didn't move.

"See you later, darling," she called.

Harold grunted in reply.

Were all teenagers like this, she wondered? She shut the door behind her and walked out to the car.

Harold only looked up when he heard the door close. He liked having the house to himself. He could be free from Aunt Enid's attention, from her solicitous interruptions. Outside he heard her starting the car. He waited a few minutes then got up and went into the kitchen. He looked out the window. The car was gone. He took a bottle of Coke out of the refrigerator and opened it. Grabbing a large bag of Fritos he went back into the living room. He was prepared for a relaxing evening. Alone with some good food and the TV.

Bilko had finished and *What's My Line* was beginning. He never understood why anyone would want to watch this. Four old farts trying to guess what someone did for a living. Who the hell cares, thought Harold. He bent down and switched channels. Dinah Shore was on Channel 4. That wasn't much better. Worse. A current affairs program was on ABC and on Channel 5 there was the news. He never watched the news. Boring stuff. He turned off the set.

Back in his room he put on a Muddy Waters record, *I'm Your Hoochie Coochie Man*, Chess, 1953, blue and silver, flip side *She's So Pretty*. It was one that Alvin had insisted he buy. He hadn't particularly liked it at the time. He asked Alvin what a Hoochie Coochie Man was. The blind man had laughed, his lopsided mouth opening to expose brown-blotched gums and the scars on his face twisting like snakes. Harold shuddered. Alvin felt for him and dug his fingers into the boy's soft forearm.

"A regular loverman, little piss-ant. Sure enough, a regular nigra lov-er man! That's right. Yeah it is. Shee-it! You'll find out about it one day soon coming. You surely will."

He laughed again, a trail of spit landing on the leg of Harold's pants. Harold didn't like it when Alvin grabbed hold of him and laughed his busted-mouth, blind-man's laugh. He liked Alvin's airborne slobber even less.

He lay down on his bed, closed his eyes and listened. The hard blues beat, the gravelly, but somehow sweet and slow, low-down sound of Muddy Waters and the shrill phrasing of Little Walter's harmonica helped clear his mind.

However, it wasn't long before it began to fill up again.

It had been over a month since he had bought a record. Maybe Aunt Enid would let him go up to LA on the bus. He could stay with one of his friends. But, where was he going to get the money? He only had a few dollars left after the drive-in. At home his father had given him a weekly allowance and on Saturday afternoons he had helped out in Mr. Jenkins' grocery store filling shelves, sweeping the floor, cleaning the windows, delivering groceries and listening to Mr. Jenkins' complaints about Ralphs and Safeway and his stories about the war. The complaints were always the same — the big monoply chain stores were making it impossible for the little guy to make a decent living. The stories were always the same too.

"You should have seen 'em, Harold. Stinking dead Japs were all over the place. The islands were just crawling with 'em. In the trees, in the foxholes, behind bushes, all over the place. Smelled terrible. I remember that smell. Rotting things. Dead bodies. Terrible darn smells."

He didn't miss the afternoons with Mr. Jenkins, but he did miss the money. Could he ask Aunt Enid for an allowance? Could he find a Saturday job in Palm Springs?

He reached under the bed and pulled out a rumpled copy of *Playboy*. He could feel his erection starting before he found the centerfold page. He put his hand down the front of his pants to help it along. He thought about the girl at the drive-in. She seemed to like him. He tried to imagine her without any clothes on, but all he could see was a mouth full of metal-clad teeth. He saw his aunt, her breasts swinging heavily as she climbed out of the pool, nipples puckered from the water. He tried to concentrate on the girl in the magazine. Angie, who was 22 years old, liked horses and riding motorcycles. Things that rubbed up between her legs. She had long smooth legs, large firm breasts. Before he could get very far into his masturbatory fantasy, the doorbell rang.

He sat up and hurriedly shoved the magazine under the bed. He hoped it wasn't Earl. He had escaped relatively lightly from the drive-in and he had no intention of going out with them again. He sort of liked Earl, but his friends were trouble. They were just the kind of boys his mother was always warning him about.

"Gangsters, Harold. Gangsters I'm telling you. Nogoodnicks. You want to end up a garbageman, a ditch digger or a gas station attendant? Huh? Do you?"

He didn't need the warnings, and anyway, it wasn't the future that worried Harold, it was the potentially violent present. He had steered well clear. Until Palm Springs that is. He hadn't worked anything out, but he would have to think of some way to avoid Earl and his friends.

The doorbell rang again. He got up, went into the living room and opened the front door. Harold relaxed. It wasn't Earl, just an old man. Harold turned on the outside light. The old man squinted into the sudden glare, put up his hand to shield his eyes.

"Mrs. Carlson in?" the man asked.

"Not home," replied Harold, starting to close the door.

"I see."

The old man smiled warmly at Harold. Harold noticed that his two front teeth were broken. They had jagged edges and were yellowed like old piano keys. Grey stubble on his face, a wide-lapelled suit creased and dusty, as if he had been walking slowly down a country road on a hot day. He wore a tie and what seemed to be a fairly clean white shirt, his sparse grey hair shiny wet and combed straight back. An effort to look respectable. It didn't really work. Harold looked at his shoes. His father always said that that was the first thing a salesman did when sizing up a customer.

"If you got clean shoes, Harry, you're a good bet and they treat you decent. It means you take pride. You know what I mean? Dirty shoes? They don't want to know from dirty shoes. You just remember that, son."

Harold did remember. Surprisingly, by the saleman's test the old man was apparently a good bet. There was a little dust, but his brown wing-tips were highly polished. So much for that piece of advice, thought Harold.

"You her son?" asked the man.

"Nephew," answered the boy uneasily.

The old man's smile broadened. He took a step closer and held out his arms as if he were going to grab him. Harold backed away quickly and slammed the door shut.

He leaned against the closed door, his heart pounding in his throat and listened. He could hear the old man laughing. The laugh soon became a cough, deep and hacking. It went on for some time.

"Please, son, open the door," the old man pleaded breathlessly.

He was not about to open the door. The old man looked dangerous. There were a lot of crazy people around, especially in the desert.

"Go away now," Harold yelled. "Or I'm going call the cops."

"Please, just open the door. I'm a sick man. Please, I need a drink of water."

As if to illustrate his point he began to cough again.

"Who are you?" shouted Harold. "Wadda you want?"

"Open the door and I'll tell you. I can't talk though a closed door, yelling like a fishwife out here in the street. You want all the neighbors should hear? Come on son, I'm not going to hurt you, I promise. Cross my heart."

Harold set the chain and only then did he open the door. He looked out through the two-inch gap. The old man was standing about three feet away leaning against a metal post, still smiling, his face sickly pale in the direct light. He began to pat the dust off his suit coat and pants.

"Damned desert gets all over you, doesn't it?"

Deep lines cut down the sides of his face, the collar and cuffs of his shirt were frayed, the suit was too big and hung lopsided from one shoulder. Everything about him, except his shoes, seemed second-hand and off-center. Even his nose had been broken and pushed over to one side.

"OK," said Harold, "What?"

"Can I come in a minute, maybe? Talk inside."

Aunt Enid would kill him if he let this strange, dirty old guy into her house.

"No," Harold said, "can't do it, sorry."

The old man shook his head and smiled ruefully.

"Tell me something, will you please? Is this the way to treat your own grandfather?"

* * *

Abe Cohen sat at the dining room table cradling a mug of coffee. His hands shook slightly. Now that he was inside Harold realized that not only did he look strange, he also stank. A raw mixture of cigarette butts, whiskey, rank body odor and piss. Harold opened the sliding glass door to the patio and tried to find a position upwind from his grandfather.

"Did you know you had a grandfather, Harold? Did the girls tell you about me?"

"Sort of, um, I mean, not really very much I guess."

How could he tell him that his mother only mentioned him when she was very upset and then only to use him as a curse, a doom-shrouded vision of Harold's certain future.

"A bum, Harold. You want to be like him, a rotten, no-good bum? Just keep it up. I'm warning you, you just keep it up like you're doing and you'll see how it turns out."

Harold knew the story of how her father had abandoned them during a cold New York winter. How she and her sister had had to leave school and go out to work. How her mother had suffered. The Depression, always it was the Depression. Every time he complained about something he got the Depression.

"Kids today, they don't know how lucky. When I was your age, Harold I..."

And now, here he was, across the table from him sipping coffee. The *Curse of the Cohens* as his father called him. This crazed-looking old man was actually his grandfather, the only blood relative he had besides Aunt Enid. Harold studied him closely, but he saw only an old drifter in hand-me-down clothes. Why had he come? What did he want? What was Aunt Enid going to say?

"Well, listen, it was a long time ago," Abe said with a shrug. "I had to go look for work, if you hear what I'm saying. In the Depression it was. You've heard about the Depression? Yeah, well it was very tough to find a job. It hasn't been easy for me, Harold. You can write that down in your book. No, not easy for an old man. Do you think I could have another cup of coffee, Harold?"

"Sure."

The old man crossed his legs. One sock rolled down to reveal a hairless ankle covered in liver spots and patterned with finely broken blood vessels. He scratched vigorously at his arms, his chest. It was as if he wanted to tear off skin. Harold imagined lice.

He got up and went into the kitchen.

"Maybe you have some bread and cheese?" the old man wheezed pathetically. "I haven't eaten since I left LA. Not that I'm very hungry or anything like that. Used to like to eat. Sort of lost interest somehow. But a little something, you know what I'm saying? I won't say no to a little something."

From the kitchen Harold watched him sizing up the living room, assessing how his daughter was doing. He continued to scratch himself. Harold began to itch. He'd never seen a lice. Or was it louse, like with mouse?

"You want it grilled?" he asked.

"Thanks, that would be nice."

Like with *mice*, Harold thought, putting the pieces of bread in the toaster. When they popped up he peeled off two slices of Kraft cheese and dropped them between the toast. He put it in the oven and turned on the grill. Harold knew instinctively that his grandfather had not just dropped in to say hello and get a bite to eat. Something far more serious was about to happen. He couldn't quite get it in focus, but he was increasingly uneasy.

Maybe It Wasn't Necessary...

"You know, Harold, I can't say I like the desert. Not what I've seen of it anyway. Coming down on the train it seemed so empty, so far away from anywhere. You hear what I'm saying? You like it here, in the desert?"

"It's OK," Harold said, not wanting to give too much away.

Harold put the grilled cheese sandwich on the table in front of his grandfather. The old man bent his head and sniffed it. Harold thought he was going to complain, maybe send it back like his mother used to do when they went out to eat. If it wasn't just the way she wanted it, back it went.

"You call this medium rare? I specifically asked for medium rare, didn't I, Norman?"

Going out to eat with his parents made Harold very nervous. Once he had even complained about it. Once.

"Whose side are you on, Harold? The cook's or your own mother?"

There was no answer to that.

The old man picked up the sandwich and began to eat.

"How did I find you?" he asked, the words edging out around bits of half chewed sandwich. "I bet you've been dying to ask. Huh? An old man like me, how did I find one of my daughters and my grandson? Huh? Ha ha!"

He seemed very pleased with himself. Harold didn't reply. What could he say? Abe tapped the side of his head with his forefinger.

"Smart, that's how, the old man is still smart. You believe that, don't you, Harold?"

He took a large bite from the sandwich.

"By the way, how's your dear mother?"

Harold sat down heavily.

"Don't you know?"

"Know? Know what?" said Abe, slowly placing the half-eaten sandwich on the plate.

"There was a car accident... on the freeway, about a month or so ago, and..." his voice caught. "My father too."

"It was bad? Very bad?" Abe asked.

Harold nodded.

Abe's body went slack, his eyes dulled.

"Oh my God. Oh my God," he said in a soft abstracted voice.

"Sylvia, my poor little Sylvia. My little girl. So pretty. All these years. All these years gone..."

Harold felt a lump in his throat, felt the tears coming. He fought against it. He wasn't going to cry in front of a stranger, even if he was his grandfather. He didn't understand why, but he felt that to give the old man any kind of emotional opening would be a mistake.

"I never thought," said Abe, staring down at his feet, shaking his head slowly from side to side. "You don't think about that, do you? They shouldn't die before you do, your children. No, they shouldn't. And, the worst is that she died thinking bad thoughts about me. Bad thoughts. I never had the chance, you see. To explain that is. I could have. Sure, I could. Lots of things to tell her. To explain about what happened. Never in time. That's the story of my life, never in time. You hear what I'm saying, Harold? Old Abe Cohen, never in damn time."

He looked outside, staring dead-eyed at a many-armed Joshua tree outlined in the moonlit garden.

"Don't like the desert much," he muttered to himself. "Hot in the day, spooky at night. Full of snakes and lizards. Too much dust. Dust, all over dust. No place for a normal person."

He rubbed his eyes, put the mug to his lips.

"You don't have anything a little stronger? A drop of whiskey or maybe some brandy? I've had quite a shock, you know. Quite a shock for an old man."

Harold walked over to the cocktail trolley in the living room and picked-up a half-empty bottle of J&B.

"That's alright," said Abe, when he saw Harold with a glass. "The cup is OK."

The old man watched with a measuring eye as Harold poured the whiskey.

He put his hand on the boy's arm.

"That's OK, Harold," he said with a smile and a wink, "why don't you just leave the bottle?"

Abe took a long drink. It caught halfway down and he started to cough. Again and again his body shuddered as if he were being punched. A thin stream of saliva escaped from the corner of his mouth. After a minute or so the attack passed and he flopped back in the chair exhausted, his eyes red and watery. He wiped his mouth with the back of his sleeve and took another drink from the cup. This time it went down without incident.

The whiskey diluted his grief, put a spark back in his eyes.

"Sorry, Harold, sorry. Can't seem to shake this damn cough. Maybe the dry air would be good for it. Desert got to be good for something. Right? How old are you, boy?"

"Almost sixteen."

"Almost sixteen," repeated Abe. "Have a drink with me?"

"No. No thanks."

"OK, don't mind if I have another, do you?"

"No."

Abe filled the coffee mug with whiskey. There was hardly any left in the bottle. He patted the pockets of his jacket.

"You don't have a cigarette, do you? I seem to be fresh out."

"No, sorry. Don't smoke."

"Sure, kid, and a good thing too. Terrible habit, terrible. You just listen to these old lungs of mine."

Harold listened to the splutter and sucking rasp as his grandfather demonstrated the evils of tobacco by trying to breathe in.

"Uh... maybe there's a long butt in that ashtray over there? Wadda you think?"

He pointed to the coffee table by the couch. Harold got the ashtray and brought it over to his grandfather. Delicately the old man chose a cigarette which had been stubbed out. He smiled with satisfaction as he smoothed it between his fingers. He noticed Harold watching him and shrugged.

"Just to see me right. It's an emergency. You understand about that, don't you Harold?"

He pulled a book of matches from one of the side pockets of his jacket.

"Now matches are another story. Always have 'em. Lots of matches. Never can have too many. Man gets cold, wants to see in the dark, light a cigarette what does he need? Right, matches. Fire, Harold, fire. It's what sets us apart from all the other animals. Of course, then again you could say it was pants."

"Pants?" squeaked Harold, suddenly outflanked.

The old man leaned forward so his face was a few inches from Harold's. His voice took on a soft, confiding tone. The whiskey fumes from his breath brought tears to Harold's eyes.

"Sure, pants... or hats or rubber gloves, any of that stuff. You know what I'm saying? You ever seen a racoon wearing pants, a hat and rubber gloves? No, you have not and you never will either, not this side of the grave anyway."

Noticing the bewilderment on Harold's face, the old man slapped the table and began to laugh. He was soon doubled up, coughing once again. But, during the entire bout, as his body twisted and shook, flailed and rattled, the cigarette never left the corner of his mouth. When he finally recovered he lit the cigarette and inhaled deeply.

Harold braced himself for another coughing attack, but nothing happened.

"Ah, that's more like it," said Abe. "You don't have much to say for yourself, do you Harold?"

He paused and took another sip from the mug.

"Don't look like your dear mother, do you? Your father maybe?"

"No, not really," Harold replied.

"Red hair? Rachel's mother had grey hair, never knew her father. Maybe she had red hair before the grey hair. Probably explains it. From Poland she was. Emma Wilna, a regular terror. Didn't like me at all. No one was good enough for her precious Rachel, no one. Damn old cow. She was such a misery she up and died the week after we got married. Can you imagine that? Dead as a Polish herring. Nothing was ever really the same between me and Rachel after that. Never could figure out what it all meant."

He tipped back the mug and then looked closely at Harold.

"Yeah, red hair from Poland."

He patted Harold's thick shoulder.

"A grandson. How about that? Old Abe Cohen has got himself a grandson. We're going to be good friends, right Harold? Good, *good* friends."

"Sure," said Harold, moving his chair closer to the open patio door. "Sure we are."

* * *

As soon as she pulled into the driveway she knew something was wrong. It was after twelve o'clock and Harold was outside waiting for her. Caught in the headlights he shifted impatiently from one foot to the other. She opened the car door and got out hurriedly.

"Harold darling, what ever's the matter?"

"I...um, there's someone come. I don't know..."

"Who? Who's come?"

It couldn't be Archie, she thought. He'd only called a couple of days before and he said a week or so. What if he came early as a surprise? Oh, God no!

Harold swallowed hard and looked at his aunt's feet.

"He says he's sorta your father or something."

Enid stepped back as if she had been slapped. Her legs buckled and she had to lean against the car to keep from falling over.

"Are you sure? Are you sure that's what he said?"

"Positive. Abe Cohen he said his name was."

Abe Cohen. God, thought Enid, a ghost, a real live ghost. How many years had it been? Twenty-five. Twenty-five years. Why now after all that time? Her father. Although she had been bitter about what he had done, she had never shared Sylvia's intense feeling against him. It seemed that her sister's hate was more than enough for both of them. Anyway, she had been only ten years old, her father's favorite, and was hurt rather than angry when he went away. She would lie in bed at night and think how he would make his fortune and return to them with lots of presents, take them off in an automobile to a big house in the country. By the time she was fifteen and he had been gone for over five years, she would conjure up that particular fantasy less and less. Soon it faded completely. Now finally he had returned.

"Where is he?" she asked Harold.

"Inside," he said, turning away and moving slowly towards the house.

She sensed the Harold was keeping something from her, but realized that it was not worth trying to pry it out of him. She followed him into the house.

* * *

She heard him and smelled him before she saw him. He had fallen asleep in a chair by the dining room table, head thrown back, arms dangling at his side, mouth wide open showing off his yellowed, broken teeth. With each in-breath he wheezed deep in his chest. On the out-breath he snored. The noise and the smell seemed to fill up the room.

"He's been like that for the last couple of hours," explained Harold, with a nervous laugh. "I've been sitting outside by the pool."

Ignoring Harold, Enid walked slowly across the room. She inclined her head to one side then another as she approached the figure slumped in the chair, trying from different angles and distances to recognize her father. She couldn't, even up close. It was a stranger, a total stranger. A shabbily dressed, unshaven, filthy old man, a bum, one of those guys they shoveled off New York's Canal Street every morning. It was not the person for whom she had waited all those years before. Not someone who would bring her presents or take her away. She hurried past him out onto the darkened patio.

"It's not him," she said quietly, shaking her head back and forth, "It's not him. Not my father. No. A mistake, it's some kind of mistake."

She took a deep breath. It caught as a sob high up in her throat. Standing by the pool, her arms tightly crossed, holding herself, she wept silently.

Harold watched her from the doorway. He had expected her to take charge when she returned, to explain everything to him, to sort things out. He had been depending on her. Now she stood with her back to him, shoulders trembling. Although she didn't make a sound, Harold knew she was crying and it frightened him.

"Aunt Enid?" he called softly.

She didn't answer. He took a couple of steps and called again. Behind him in the house Abe Cohen wheezed and snored.

"It's OK, Harold darling. I'll be alright in a minute," she said after a few moments. "I've just had a shock. Close the door, will you dear?"

She sat down by the edge of the pool and stared into the dark water. It didn't help her get a clearer picture of what she was feeling. She took off her shoes, put her feet into the cool water, leaned back on her elbows and looked up. The sky was moonlight bright. The night was clear and hot, the air completely still, and out by the pool the crickets were busy rustling and buzzing.

"Harold, what do you say we have a midnight swim? Just the two of us. How about it?"

"Uh, no thanks, Aunt Enid. I don't have any trunks or anything."

"Come on, it's dark. You won't get a sunburn and you can swim in your underwear. That's what I'm going to do. I promise, dear, I won't look. Come on, Harold, it will cool us off and do us both some good."

He didn't want to go swimming, especially not alone with Aunt Enid. By the light coming from the house behind him he could see that she was already taking off her clothes. Although he couldn't see her very clearly, his penis began to harden with the memory of the time he had spied her swimming naked.

"No! Please, not now," he muttered to himself, desperately trying to conjure up non-erotic, deflating images.

But, the more he tried, the more erotic the images became and the less his control over his growing erection.

"What did you say, Harold?"

"Nothing. Just, uh... nothing."

"Get us a couple of towels, will you dear?"

Harold went inside and got the towels from the closet in the hall, and then like someone terrified of heights but feeling himself drawn inexorably towards the edge of the cliff he went out to the pool. There was a pile of clothes on a chair. He could just make out Aunt Enid's head moving slowly through the water. Her body was submerged in the darkness.

"Thanks, darling. Come on in, it's lovely, really it is."

Harold looked back towards the house but there was no help there, only a snoring, passed-out grandfather, his gape-mouthed face and one trailing arm just visible through the open door.

"No," said Harold. "I gotta go back..."

"OK, OK, I'm not going to force you, but at least sit down and talk to me for a few minutes, Harold. You can do that, can't you?"

Harold hesitated. He couldn't very well refuse to talk to his aunt. Moving her clothes carefully onto the ground he sat down in the chair. Aunt Enid swam over to the side of the pool nearest to him. She laid her folded arms on the edge, the rest of her body remained hidden by the water.

"So, tell me what he said, Harold. Everything he said."

Harold told her as much as he could remember. After he finished Enid ducked her head into the water, brought it up and shook it. Harold caught a glimpse of her breasts moving through the water. He quickly turned away and crossed his legs.

"Did he say why he's here? What he wants?"

"No. Not really."

"What do you mean 'not really'?" she snapped impatiently.

"I mean no he didn't," Harold replied stolidly, suddenly recognizing his mother in Aunt Enid's voice.

"Or how he found us?"

"No."

"Well he can't stay here, can he?" she exclaimed angrily. "I'm not running a goddamned hotel! I've got no more room and that's that."

As soon as she'd said it, Enid realized she shouldn't have. She felt Harold stiffen. Slowly and delicately, so as not to disturb anything, he got up from his chair. He didn't look at her.

"I, um... gotta go to sleep now," he said distantly, walking back towards the house.

"Harold darling," she called after him. "You know I didn't mean..."

He wasn't listening. Head down he made for the open door. Stepping inside, he quietly pulled it shut behind him.

* * *

Enid got out of the pool and wrapped a towel around herself. She thought of going after Harold, but decided not to. She couldn't face trying to talk to him. To make contact with her oversized nephew was a major effort and she didn't feel up to a major effort just then. And, anyway, why did she have to explain herself to him? She had taken him in, was looking after him, trying to love him. What could she explain?

Slowly she walked back towards the house. She stopped at the door and looked inside. Her father was in the exact position he had been in when she first came home, only with the door shut she couldn't hear him or smell him. Could she just leave him there and go to bed? She slid the door open and went inside.

Refreshed from her swim and no longer unprepared, she sat down across the table and studied the old man more carefully, more dispassionately. The skin on his face was greyish-yellow and hung in little sacks from his cheeks. On the tip of his bashed-in nose a few dark hairs bristled. His breathing was uneven and very labored. Then she noticed his hands. The skin was flaky white, almost translucent. A thread of saliva hung from the side of his mouth. As she watched, it detached itself and plopped onto his shirt, adding to the damp stain already there.

God! thought Enid shuddering, he's a total mess. He must have got his clothes from the Salvation Army. He looks eighty, but can't be more than sixty-five at the most. What's happened to him in the last twenty-five years? Where's he been? What's he been doing? And what the hell has brought him here to me? Why now?

Whatever the reason, she knew she would have to get rid of him and quickly. She had an obligation to Harold, there was no getting around that, but not to this man. She felt absolutely no duty to this stranger who had abandoned her all those years ago and had never come back.

Archie was going to arrive soon. He might just understand about Harold, but not about Abe Cohen. Why should he? She didn't understand about Abe Cohen.

* * *

Harold stepped carefully by his sleeping grandfather and went to his room. He closed the door behind him and sat down heavily on the bed. He stared at the roses on the wall without seeing them.

"I'm not running a goddamned hotel! I've got no more room and that's that."

It was the first time Aunt Enid had shown any anger towards his being there. He hadn't thought about what she might feel when he moved in with her. She was his aunt and a grown-up. That was all. He had assumed that she sort of had to take care of him, and anyway she seemed so concerned with pleasing him that it never occurred to Harold that she might be resentful. And that wasn't fair. He couldn't help being there, could he? Tears of injustice and self-pity blurred the roses. He rubbed his eyes with the back of his hand.

Absentmindedly he picked a record out of one of the cardboard boxes on the floor. He turned it over and over in his hands. He didn't look at the label. After a couple of minutes he put it back in the box, not bothering to get it in the right order. Watson, Johnny Guitar next to Mayfield, Percy.

The old man. His grandfather. How could there be any connection between them? He wasn't even a regular grandfather. Not kindly, white-haired, wise, or any of those things, like in the stories about grandfathers. And, he clearly meant to stay. Where? There were only two bedrooms. Harold knew the old man was going to make life more difficult for him. Aunt Enid was already on the warpath against intruders. The old man and him.

He bent over and untied his shoes, kicked them off and lay down on the bed, his arms behind his head.

The skeletel-thin ocotillo outside his window looked sinister in the moonlight. If he turned away or closed his eyes he knew it would rip through the screen, snake into the room and wrap its white thorny arms around his neck. Strangle him, suck him dry. In the morning Aunt Enid would find a husk-dry shell on the bed. It would fall into dust at her touch, just like in *The Invasion of the Body Snatchers*.

Palm Springs. It wasn't working out very well at all for him. Aunt Enid's constant fussing and pawing, sunstroke, caught up with thugs at the drive-in, and now this smelly old man. He felt more trapped than ever. Everywhere he turned something unexpected found him. He longed for the expected.

Risking the ocotillo's attack, he closed his eyes.

In LA he used to go with his friends to the La Brea tar pits. Later he found out that *la brea* meant tar in Spanish. The Tar Pits tar pits. Really stupid. Once his friend Ruben found a skinny stray cat. The opportunity was too good to pass up. They stuffed it in a gunny sack and threw the sack over the chain-link fence into the middle of one of the tar pits. Immediately the sack began to sink. The brown fabric shook and billowed violently in all directions as hissing and yowling the cat tried to escape. The harder it fought the more the sack stuck fast and the deeper it sank into the tar. Harold and the other boys watched the struggle in awed silence, frightened and ashamed of what they had done, yet thrilled at the same time.

"Hey you boys," someone had shouted, "what do you think you're doing there?"

It was one of the park attendants. He came hurrying over towards them. He was wearing a brown uniform and had a long-handled rake in one hand. They ran, not looking back, robbed of the final scene.

Harold often wondered if the park guy had reached the cat before it was sucked under.

... After All.

It seemed as if she had spent the entire night trying to get to sleep. She would doze off fitfully and then wake up again. 2:00, 3:30, 4:15. Everytime she looked at the luminous dial of the Baby Ben on the bedside table it was too early to get up. Finally, the sound of the patio door opening woke her up. She looked at the clock again. It was 6:00, late enough to stop fighting and get out of bed. But, what was Harold doing up so early? Then she remembered about her father and immediately was wide awake, her stomach churning.

Hurriedly she showered and dressed, all the time rehearsing what she would say to him. What do you say to a father you haven't seen since you were ten years old? A father who walked away without so much as a good-bye and left you and your mother and sister without a penny. Tell him what a bastard he had been? What a hard time her mother had had? No. What was the point after twenty-five years? He looked to be beyond recriminations, and in any case, she didn't want a scene. There was always,"Hi, nice to see you." No, that didn't sound right, and anyway, it wasn't particularly nice to see him. On the other hand, she was curious. She had to admit that it would be interesting to talk to him, find out things. But, if she did that, if she asked him about himself wouldn't he take that as a sign that she was being friendly and forgiving? She didn't want to put out signs like that. He would read them as "stay awhile." Right. She would say how she was glad to see him, and... Glad? Why not a white lie? It wouldn't hurt. OK. She was glad to see him, but no, she was sorry, as he could see it was a very small place. And there was Harold to think about. He would have to find somewhere else, she would tell him. Was there a Y.M.C.A.? Surely not in Palm Springs. In Indio? If she gave him some money would he go away? How much cash did she have in the house? Maybe money wasn't such a great idea. It might just encourage him to hang around, like putting out a saucer of milk for a stray cat. Muttering out loud to herself, she paced slowly back and forth across the small bathroom. Suddenly she caught sight of her face in the mirror. She stopped.

Is this what he's done to me already, she thought, seeing the lines of tension across her forehead, the corners of her mouth pulled down tight. Opening and closing her mouth as wide as she could, she tried to relax. It didn't work, and as she watched, the lines seemed to etch their way deeper into her skin.

"Holy God in Heaven!" she shouted at the face in the mirror. "You haven't even spoken to him yet and already you've put on ten years."

Shadow, liner, mascara, a touch of powder, lipstick. If she stood back a step or two, she didn't look so bad. She tried to smile. It looked as if she was in pain.

The patio door was wide open. It made her angry. She was always so careful to close it so that the flies, spiders, beetles, and all the other things that crawled or slithered out of the desert wouldn't get into the house. The old man had been there five minutes and had opened the floodgates. They'd be everywhere by now. In the drapes, under the sink, in the closets. Eating things, spinning webs, waiting to drop in her hair, to run across her face in the middle of the night. Archie hated bugs. She'd have to call in the exterminators. Damn!

He was sitting in *her* chair by the pool, his back to the house. His shoes were off and he was dangling his feet in *her* water. She stepped out onto the patio, sliding the door closed behind her. Taking a deep breath, she walked towards him. The cement felt cool under her bare feet. He didn't move until she was standing next to him.

"That's good," he said, turning around and looking up at her. "Very good. An early riser just like your father."

"Good morning," she said, trying to keep any emotion out of her voice.

"Of course, good morning!" he said, struggling up from the chair. "After all this time, good morning, my little girl! Good morning!"

He looked at her, his eyes moving up and down, cataloguing, assessing.

"Not my little girl, huh? My big girl! Sure, all lovely and grown up. So lovely she is!"

Smiling broadly, he stepped forward and put out his arms to embrace her. Seeing her stiffness and her cold stare, he stopped. His arms hung in the air for a second or two, then fell weakly to his sides.

"Sure," he said, with a shrug. "I understand. You don't see me for twenty years and..."

"Twenty-five years."

"Yeah, of course, twenty-five years and so maybe I shouldn't expect a big welcome. I can see that. But it was so long ago, Enid honey, so long ago and I am your father, which has gotta be worth something to you, and I've come all this way here to see you and the boy and..."

In the morning sunlight his face looked more ravaged than it had the night before. A fine patina of broken blood vessels under the grey stubble. The skin a pale yellow, like thin parchment. Wet, gelatinous eyes. A livid scar cut across his forehead. His hands trembled.

"... see how you're doing."

She sat down by the side of the pool and put her feet in the water.

"Feels good, doesn't it? Cooling," he said, settling back in the chair.

She glanced at his feet. Like his face they were yellowish and red veined, the toenails thick and a deeper yellow. Yellow seemed to be his color — skin, teeth, nails. She looked away.

"Why?" she asked, staring out into the water.

"Why? Why what?" he replied.

"Why did you come here?"

"Such a question! Why? Why did I come?"

He looked at her, but she wasn't going to help him. Finally, he gave up.

"Like I said Enid honey, to see you."

"But, why?"

He patted the pockets of his jacket.

"You don't have a smoke, do you? I seem to be fresh out."

Enid put her hand in the pocket of her blouse and found a half empty pack of Salem. She tossed them to Abe.

"Thanks. Salem, huh? Don't really care for menthol," he muttered under his breath. "You see it sort of..."

"You don't like 'em," she said through tight lips, "don't smoke 'em. That's all I've got."

"Hey, no, sure, ha, ha, don't get me wrong, Enid honey. They'll be fine, really. Just fine."

He lit a cigarette and put the pack on the ground by his chair. He inhaled deeply and began to cough. His body shook violently. After a minute the coughing stopped.

"Excuse me. First one in the morning is always like that. Old lungs are a little bit rusty, if you hear what I'm saying."

With a grating, rumbly noise he cleared his throat, expertly directing the glob of spit into the nearby bushes. Enid shuddered and looked away.

"Ah, that's better, much better. Now what was it you were asking me?"

Enid paused before answering. He was sitting too comfortably in her chair, shoes off, making himself at home. Her plan for getting rid of him was slipping away. She had to turn it all around and quickly.

"Why did you come here?" she asked in a brisk businesslike voice. "What do you want with me? From me?"

"Want? What do I want? I should want something? Isn't it enough to see your daughter and your grandson? Enid honey, we're family aren't we?"

He rolled back one sleeve and pointed at his thin naked arm. It was covered in red tracks where he had been scratching.

"Blood," he said. "You've got my blood in your veins. So does that boy. Herman isn't it?"

"Harold. His name is Harold."

"Harold, sure that's it. I knew that. Harold. So you see," he said with a shrug, "that's all there is. In the end you've only got your family. You hear what I'm saying?"

"I hear you. Loud and clear I hear you. What I want to know is why after twenty-five years all of a sudden family, blood, or whatever should become so important for you? Huh? Why so all-fired important?"

Abe took the cigarette out of his mouth and waved it in the air. With his other hand he rubbed hard at his armpit.

"You don't think it's always been important for me, Enid? You think I've got such a hard heart I didn't worry about you and Sylvia, my poor baby, and your dear mother too? No, of course not. I worried. Sure, I did. Not a day passed when I didn't think about you. Not a day, I swear to you."

He raised his right hand as if he was going to take a oath.

"On my mother's grave I swear to you."

"If you were so worried," she said her voice starting to edge up, "Why the hell didn't you just come back?"

"OK," he said leaning forward, hands on his knees. "I hear what you're saying here. Sure. But you know, I started to come back. A lot of times I started. And always, always something happened. A chance of a job in another town. The money running out. This or that. You know, it was the Depression. It was hard to find work. Real hard."

He paused, fighting to capture enough air to continue. Enid waited, fighting to harden her heart.

"You see, Enid, I was a salesman, and in the '30s it was tough for salesmen. No one had any money to buy things. So, no one wanted to employ salesmen, no matter how good you were, and I was good. You can write that down in your book. They all said that about Abe Cohen. A good salesman. Anything. Abe Cohen can sell anything. So, what did it do for me? Huh? What? Like everyone else, I had to move around looking for work. When I found it, it never lasted long. They'd get everything they could from me, suck me dry, then give me the gate. 'Sorry, Abe, we'd love to keep you on, but you know how it is.' I knew how it was. Everyone knew. I had to move on. You gotta believe me, Enid honey, I always planned to come back."

This is a mistake, she thought. I've started with the recriminations, getting involved. I have to cut him off and get him out of here. With every word he's digging himself in. The longer he stays, the more he talks, the more difficult he's going to be to move.

"Yeah, OK, OK. So what? Hard times, hard luck, whatever, you didn't come back and now you're here."

"Sure, now I'm back," he said with a big smile. "Back with the family."

"That's great," she said trying to find the right tone of voice, not wanting to get any closer to him. "But you're too late. Twenty-five years too late. Too late for your wife, my mother, who worried and worked herself to an early death. Too late for your oldest daughter, who died with nothing but bitterness for you in her heart and too late for your 'little girl' who is, as you say, 'grown up' and who did the growing up without any help from you. There's no family here for you now. No family at all."

He sat back and shook his head sadly.

"You think I wanted that?" he asked, seemingly in genuine anguish. "You can't think I wanted that? My poor Rachel and my first baby, my Sylvia, both dead?"

He took a red checked handkerchief from his back pocket and blew his nose.

"I might not be the world's greatest husband or the world's greatest father. I give you that. Not the world's greatest, but to wish them dead? Please, Enid honey, have some pity on an old man."

He gasped himself to a sudden, tearful halt. She could hear the air leaking into his chest.

Good God! This is getting worse and worse, thought Enid. He's starting to make *me* the heavy.

"OK," she said, "Now you've seen me, you've seen Harold. Now what?"

"So brisk, she is, so brisk with her father. We haven't even had a chance to talk, Enid, really talk. There's so much to tell you, to ask you. Do you think maybe we could have a cup of coffee?"

She gave him a hard look and didn't answer. She felt she'd already said too much. He looked at her searchingly.

"I don't feel so good," he said, his voice suddenly weaker and more shaky.

He began to cough again, shoulders heaving up and down with the effort. Enid got to her feet.

"OK, OK," she said impatiently, "you don't have to show me, I'll get you a cup of coffee. Cream and sugar?"

He gave a feeble smile and nodded.

"Thanks, Enid honey. You always were such a good girl. Thank you very much."

* * *

The noise from the shower woke Harold a little after 6:00. He waited until he heard Aunt Enid go out on the patio and then, as quietly as he could, he opened his door. No one was in the living room. Putting his head cautiously around the corner of the drapes he looked into the back yard. He saw them talking out by the pool. The old man was gesticulating. Aunt Enid didn't seem to be paying much attention.

If he could just stay out of the way long enough maybe Aunt Enid would get rid of the old man and he wouldn't have to get involved. Drastic action was needed. He would take a walk. It was still early enough, the sun wouldn't be a problem. He could go into town, find a cafe and have breakfast. He liked having breakfast in a restaurant. He could order scrambled eggs and hash browns. A rare treat.

"Hash browns? You must be joking, right? I don't have enough to do? What is it, you don't get enough to eat here? You can't wait to eat hash browns when you go out with your little friends?"

Why, thought Harold, had his mother refused to make hash brown potatoes? And why had she constantly talked to him in questions?

After checking that he had enough money he went through the kitchen and out of the house.

Harold was getting so he could almost tolerate the early morning desert. At least it wasn't so blistering hot. About half a mile to the west, high granite mountains rose straight up from the desert floor. In the opposite direction, far across the flat expanse of sand, was a long line of giant yellow dunes. Behind them were another range of softly-rounded mountains, dusky purple in color. Not bad to look at, he thought, but what can you do with them? In the city it was just the opposite. No pretty scenery, but always lots of things going on and, best of all, you could hide out in the crowds. There were no crowds in Palm Springs. There was nothing but dumb scenery. He kicked at the sand and then started to walk towards the center of town.

He hadn't gone more than a few yards when a horn sounded behind him. It was Earl's white pickup. Garf was in the passenger seat. The truck stopped next to him and Earl leaned out the window.

"Hey, Harold old buddy, how they hangin'?"

"Oh, yeah. Hi, guys."

"How you feeling today?" asked Earl.

"Oh," replied Harold, "I'm OK."

"Really tied one on the other night," said Earl. "We had to near pour you outta the pickup."

Earl laughed and pushed his hat back revealing a thin white strip across his forehead.

"Yeah," added Garf, craning his head around in the cab so he could see Harold, "Y'all was one fucking smashed dude and that's for damn sure."

"I guess," replied Harold.

"I reckon I ain't never seen anyone puke so much," said Earl, admiringly. "Damn me if I have."

"That's right enough," added Garf.

Harold couldn't decide whether they were complimenting him. He wanted to ask about his socks but didn't.

"You wanna ride or something?" asked Earl.

"Well, uh, dunno," said Harold, remembering his resolution to steer clear of Earl and his friends. "Just going up into town is all."

"Come on. No need to walk it. Remember what happened the last time."

"Right. Thanks."

Reluctantly, Harold went around and climbed into the truck next to Garf.

"You is one big fucking critter for sure," said the smaller boy as he slid to the middle of the seat.

"What you doing today?" asked Earl, as he put the truck in gear and started off.

"Me? Not a lot, I guess."

"Listen, me and Garf here are fixing to get something to eat then to head up to the high desert to check on some horses they got for sale. You wanna come along for the ride or what?"

He didn't really want to go, but if he stayed in town he was sure he would get tangled up in the mess between his grandfather and his aunt, and he figured that their problems weren't really his problems.

He glanced over at Earl. That he was a cowboy and liked to mess around with horses, that he drank crappy beer in crappy drive-ins and listened to hick music didn't seem to matter. Earl was so effortlessly self-confident that he just about put Harold at ease. There was a comforting kind of competence and solidness about him. Here was a guy who would survive if he got stranded in the desert and make sure you survived as well. And Harold *was* definitely stranded. He had also made up his mind that he wanted to survive, even if he had to do it with horse shit and Tennessee Ernie Ford.

Garf, however, was another matter. Edgy, with a little-man's chip on his shoulder, he made Harold nervous. He watched Earl's every move and kept in step. He could go in any direction and Harold felt he was friendly with him only because of Earl. But they weren't going to the drive-in, the Jew-loving, tatooed Jingles wasn't with them, and there were unlikely to be any confrontations with the motor-cycle gang or Tody's ex-girl's new boyfriend, the animal from the football team. "Look at some horses," that was all. Carefully Harold weighed up his options.

"Well," said Earl, "Wadda you say?"

"How long you going up there for?"

"Just for the day is all. Won't take us more than a couple a hours to get there. It's only a hoot and a holler outta Yucca Valley."

"A hoot and a holler," Harold repeated to himself. What the hell am I doing here?

"Yeah, OK, thanks a lot."

* * *

There were a few more people on Palm Canyon Drive at 6:30 in the morning than there had been the afternoon Harold took his last stroll into town. Earl parked the truck in front of the drugstore.

It was busy inside. Mostly workmen in tee shirts. There were also a couple of cops and some cowboys. The jukebox was playing. Harold couldn't identify the singer or the tune.

A white sport coat and a pink carnation
I'm all dressed up for the dance.

"Poor ol' Marty Robbins," Earl sighed, "You'd think he'd have more sense."

"You'd think," echoed Garf, glaring around the room, as if the singer was hiding somewhere in among the booths.

Harold was just glad it wasn't Pat Boone.

They sat down at the counter next to one of the cops. He was well over six feet tall and must have weighed three hundred pounds. It seemed to be all muscle. The thick hairs on his arm were like steel wool. A mug of coffee was buried in one of his hands.

"How you doing, Jim?" said Earl.

"Hey up, Little Earl," said the cop.

Harold thought the steel rivets holding the stool to the floor gave slightly as the cop swiveled to face them.

"You boys keeping your noses clean?"

"You bet," replied Earl.

"Sure you are. I know that. Say, how's Big Earl, ain't seen him around lately?"

"Oh, he's doing OK, you know, keeping outta the sun."

The cop laughed, showing a mouth full of widely spaced teeth and gold fillings.

"I know this little runt here," he said, pointing a thick finger at Garf, "But, ain't seen this one before. You new around here, boy?"

"Yes, sir," Harold managed to squeak, alarmed by the policeman's sudden interest. "Abelstein, Harold Abelstein, sir."

He could feel himself blushing.

"Polite too," said the cop, studying him more closely. "Say now, Harold Abel-*Stein*, how'd a nice boy like you get mixed up with this collection of no-account saddle-tramps?"

"I ... um... I... uh..." he stammered.

"Shit, Harold," Earl laughed "Don't pay him no never mind. He can't shoot straight anyway."

The policeman punched Earl softly on the arm and smiled good-naturedly.

"Say, you boys gonna order or what?"

It was the same blond girl who had served him before, whom he had bumped into at the drive-in. Hands on her small hips, she turned to the cop.

"You know I told you before about bothering the customers, Daddy."

"Gee, I am sorrier than hell, Gloria," he said solemnly, "I really am."

Everyone laughed, except Harold.

"Why hello again," she said seeing Harold.

She gave him a warm smile.

"You do keep turning up, don't you?"

Harold smiled weakly. He could feel the policeman's eyes on him.

"Come on, Jim," said the other cop, "let's get at it."

"Right."

The big man put down his mug and stood up. He leaned over towards the boys, looking all the time just at Harold.

"Now you boys remember what I said. I got my eye on *you*."

Harold smiled broadly at him and nodded, trying to get into the swing of things, the cut and thrust of manly insults. The cop didn't smile back.

Wrong again, thought Harold despairingly, the smile frozen on his face. He now felt more exposed than ever. It would have to be the biggest policeman in the world, the daughter of the biggest policeman in the world.

I remember the night
and the Tennessee Waltz
Now I know just how much I have lost.
I lost my little darlin'
The night they were playin'
The beautiful Tennessee Waltz.

He couldn't finish his hash browns.

As they left, Gloria ran up to him. She grabbed his arm.

"Hey now, Harold, don't you go forgetting this again."

She handed him Aunt Enid's straw hat.

* * *

Standing by the kitchen sink, Enid daydreamed as she filled the percolator, her mind restfully blank. Suddenly the water poured over the top and ran onto her hand. She shook herself awake and tried to focus once more. She turned off the faucet. He had won the first round hands down. She laughed at herself, emptied some of the water, spooned coffee into the metal filter basket, put on the top and set the pot on the stove.

One cup of coffee. I'll let him have one cup and then it's back on the road. No more questions, no more openings.

It was going badly wrong, not at all how she had planned. She was not being cool and decisive. He was making her angry and that made her feel guilty. Why the hell should I feel guilty, she thought? Because he's my father? What difference should that make? He abandoned me, for Christ sake! When I was ten years old, nothing but a little kid. What kind of father does that? Could he have really loved me? And, he thinks I should feel sorry for him? Sorry for him! After that and after what he did to Mom? She stared out the kitchen window into the street for a full minute. Hell, I do feel sorry for him!

"The bastard!" she said out loud, banging her hand against the side of the stove and almost upsetting the coffee pot.

She carried the two mugs out to the pool. Abe had taken his coat off and rolled up his sleeves.

"Thanks, Enid. That really hits the spot."

He held the mug in both hands and bent forward as he drank.

"You know, I've traveled a lot, all around the country, but never really been in the desert. When I first came out to the West Coast it was up in Washington. Had a job for a while in Clarkson, little town on the Snake River across from Lewiston. You know, Lewis and Clark? Two towns, right next to each other. Still, I suppose it's better than Kansas City and Kansas City. You hear what I'm saying?"

He paused and when Enid didn't respond he continued talking. Silence seemed to frighten him. Enid imagined it was because he couldn't sell anything when it was quiet. The only thing to do was for him to fill up the empty space.

"Well, I got off the train there, you see. Worked in a drug store. Wilson's I think it was called. Right there on the main street it was. Yeah, Wilson's Drugs. Big blue and white letters across the front. Went to Seattle for a while after that. Wasn't much work in Seattle. Rains a lot up there, you know. Nice place though."

He shook his head.

"But the desert. I don't know about the desert. Nothing but sand and wind and it's so hot and so empty. Lots and lots of empty."

He laughed to himself.

"Yeah, lots of empty. Why would anyone want to live here? You hear what I'm saying?"

Still Enid didn't answer. The old man shifted in the chair and smiled. He took another drink from the mug, licked his lips nervously.

"You know when I got off out there," he pointed vaguely north. "Off the Southern Pacific, that is, I said to myself 'Wait a minute, Abe,' I said, 'there's nothing here.' Desert all around. A little station, a couple of shacks and an old water tower. 'Where the hell is Palm Springs?' I said. Then I saw this sign. A big arrow, *Palm Springs 9 miles. Population 12,146. 1044 swimming pools. 289 hotels.* What a place, huh? What a place."

"You can't stay," she blurted out.

"If I hadn't found an... What? What did you say?"

"I said you can't stay," she repeated, feeling relieved she had finally got it out. "I don't have any room. There's only the two bedrooms. It's a small house. I'm sorry, but that's how it is."

Not looking at his daughter, Abe put his mug on the ground.

"Uh... yeah, sure," he said, suddenly cut loose from his plans and momentarily confused.

Then with careful deliberation he began to unroll one shirt sleeve.

"I can see that, Enid honey. Of course I can... But, you see, I hadn't planned really, you know, actually planned *to stay* exactly... Just sort of lay over, as it were, a couple of days maybe... you know... See you and the boy and then I..."

"I'm sorry, it can't be done. Where would I put you?"

"Right. Yeah... Well, listen, that shouldn't be a problem," he said, brightening. "I could sleep on the couch, couldn't I? I mean to say, only for a day or two, it shouldn't be such..."

Not again, she thought. I asked another question and he stepped right in. Damn it!

"No!" she shouted angrily.

The old man sat up in his chair, startled. He looked dazed, disoriented. He stared straight ahead, ran his hands back and forth along the arms of the canvas chair. She forced herself not to notice.

"No," she said more calmly. "I'm sorry, but no, definitely no. I have someone coming and ..."

"Alright, alright," he interrupted, seeming finally to give in to her. "Don't worry, I wouldn't want to upset anybody. I just thought that maybe you might be just a little happy to see your own father? Maybe a little curious? No? Not even a little?"

Enid didn't trust herself to speak. She studied the mountain, trying to lose her thoughts in the bright mirror chips of granite.

Abe let out a loud sigh. His shoulders dropped. His voice faltered, moving further away.

"No. I see. I see. Why not? Huh? Why not? That's fine. Sure, sure it is. I can live with that. I've lived with it for twenty-five years. The misunderstanding, the resentment, the rejection. Why should I expect ...?"

His voice brightened momentarily.

"But, I don't want you to feel bad about it, Enid honey. You musn't feel bad."

"I..." she began, and then clamped her mouth tight, her vision blurred by a paralyzing rage.

He gave her an understanding smile and then bent down with an old man's exaggerated caution and began to put on his socks.

Western Swing

Pioneertown was like a western movie set. The unpaved main street, called Mane Street, was lined on either side with low rough-cut wooden buildings, many with false-fronted second stories and wide porches. The Red Dog Saloon, Maggie's Feed Barn, the Gem Trader, Cecil the Barber, the Pony Express Service. The three boys walked down the center of the wide street which, except for a few tumbleweeds, was empty.

"It's like an old ghost town," said Harold in a hushed voice.

"Yeah," replied Earl, "sort of is. They built it about ten years ago. Wanted to make movies here. Made some, not many though. Never panned out somehow."

As they passed the Golden Stallion, a large single-story building at the corner of the street, a small Chinese man wearing a white shirt and a stetson hat stepped out onto the veranda. He smiled and nodded to the boys. Earl touched the brim of his hat.

"Jew," Earl said, shortly, as if explaining something.

Garf laughed.

A cold shiver snaked down Harold's back, his stomach tightened. "Jew?" Did he hear him right? Jew? What did Earl mean? He didn't see how it was possible.

"Uh, wasn't that guy sort of Chinese?" asked Harold tentatively.

"What? Him? Oh, yeah, sure," replied Earl, "Chinese. You like Chinese food?"

"It's OK," said Harold, trying to figure out what Earl was leading up to.

But, if he was leading up to anything Harold never found out what it was.

They reached the end of the street. About a hundred yards further on was a large corral. Three horses stood quietly at the far end. Earl put one foot on a lower rail and leaned his arms on the top of the fence.

"You see a pinto mare?" Earl asked Garf.

The smaller boy took up the same posture as his friend, but had to stretch awkwardly to reach the higher part of the corral fence.

"No. I don't see nothing. Oh, yeah, wait a minute. Look, she's behind the grey."

He pointed.

"You see her there?"

A tall broadshouldered man wearing a full cowboy rig, boots and spurs, hat and an oversized silver belt buckle, came up behind them.

"Howdy, boys, can I help you with something? Oh, hey there, Little Earl, didn't recognize you right off."

"Chester," said Earl, putting out his hand.

"Big Earl OK?" asked the man, pumping the boy's hand.

"Yeah, he's getting on just fine and dandy."

Earl didn't introduce the other boys.

Harold reached up and nervously fingered his hat. Earl had said he had better wear one if he didn't want to get sunstroke again. When Harold had complained that his aunt's hat made him look ridiculous, Garf had taken his pocketknife and cut off the bits of frayed straw.

"Make it look sorta like a fucking sombrero," he said, putting the hat on Harold's head.

"Don't worry," said Earl, "it's just fine. You look like a redheaded Mex."

"Sure he does. El Colorado Grande," laughed Garf, pleased with himself, "Hey Earl! How about that, huh? El Colorado Grande! Fucking A!"

Harold prayed that the new nickname wouldn't stick. He didn't want a Mexican nickname.

He felt self-conscious about the hat, but his skin was still tender. He wore it.

"You come about them horses?" asked Chester, casting a sidelong look at Harold.

"Yep."

"Well, lets go over there and you can have a look-see."

They walked around the outside of the corral until they came to where the horses stood. After a few minutes the man turned to Earl.

"Well, wadda you think?"

"Not bad," said Earl, speculatively.

There was another few minutes of silence.

"Like I told Big Earl, we been using 'em for dude riding. Gentle as hell, they are. Even the little kids can ride 'em. How many is it your dad's thinking to buy?"

"Two, maybe all three. You got some saddles we could throw on? Like to ride 'em around some, if that's alright?"

"Sure thing, Little Earl. You gotta see what you're buying, don't you? Come on over to the tack room and I'll get you all fixed up."

God, thought Harold. I'm not going to have to actually ride a horse. Please, no! He remembered Pony Land. He hadn't been on a horse since he was six years old. He hadn't wanted to be.

Harold sighed. Cornered again. Out of one into another. It was never ending. How long would it take before he found the balance again. It hadn't been easy in Los Angeles, but he had done it. He'd got the record *shtik* down to an art. He had worked out all his moves. Here in the desert the moves were always being worked out by someone else. He took off the hat and wiped his sleeve across his forehead.

Earl had said *looking*, he hadn't said anything about *riding*, but then Earl didn't say much, didn't explain things. It was as if he expected Harold instinctively to understand what was going on. Harold didn't, but he understood enough to know he couldn't ask.

It had to be something about the desert, he thought. Too hot to talk much. Maybe the heat and all the empty space makes people go right off-center. Or, maybe they were that way to begin with and that's why they wind up in the desert, like that Jewish Chinese cowboy.

Chester led them to a small wooden shed not far from the corral. He opened the door.

"You take what all you need, boys," he said, standing to one side. "I'll go round 'em up for you."

Earl and Garf went in. Harold didn't know what to do. Chester stared at him, waiting. Feeling uncomfortable, Harold followed the others inside.

Western Swing

It was dark and musty hot in the shed. It smelled of leather and horse sweat. About a dozen saddles sat on braced two-by-fours which stuck out from the walls. There were also bridles, halters, spurs, curry combs and stiff brushes, a pair of chaps, an opened and dried-out can of saddle soap, a couple of coiled ropes and various lengths of leather strapping. A thin strip of yellow flypaper dotted with black specks hung from the center of the ceiling. It spun slowly in the still air. Harold heard a muted buzzing and looking more closely he saw a large blue-green fly, its feet stuck fast, fighting to escape. He knew that it had no chance.

"Here, Harold," said Earl, "you grab on to this one."

Earl picked up a saddle and set it in Harold's arms.

"But I..." Harold protested, grunting at the sudden weight.

"Oh yeah," said Earl, "I forgot you're going to need these as well."

He added a stiff red and white saddle blanket and a bridle, smacking them down onto the saddle.

"Now you're all set, partner."

"Listen, Earl, you know, I never..."

"Hey, I know that, Harold. Don't fret now, I'll show you how it's all done. Come on now, you gotta be learning this sometime."

Harold didn't see why.

Back at the corral Chester had haltered the horses and tied them to the fence rail.

Earl checked each horse carefully, looking at teeth and eyes, running his hands up and down legs, inspecting hooves. Then he and Garf put on the saddles and bridles, adjusted the stirrups and checked the cinches.

"OK, Harold, old son," said Earl, "Ready to mount up? You can take this big bay here."

Harold fought to quiet the fluttering in his stomach. He tightened his jaw, tightened the cheeks of his ass and nodded, trying to adopt the accepted hard-eyed expression. Tough guy western cool. Man of few words. Resourceful, like the masked rider of the plains. Laconic, sure-footed and ready for anything.

He strolled over to the right side of the horse. The others watched him, saying nothing.

When he got right up next to it, could smell it, see its muscles twitch, Harold realized with a jolt what an enormous animal a horse actually was. It was at least twenty times bigger than any dog, and he was scared to death of dogs. Holding down his terror as best he could Harold reached up tentatively and grabbed the pommel. The horse snorted and tossed its head. Harold let go and stepped back hurriedly. All his fears were coming home. He wanted to run. Instead he farted, a loud, half-squeezed-back double report which sounded like the distress call of wild goose.

"Holy shit, Big Red!" shouted Garf, "you're after taking the seat out of your fucking pants!"

"Or scaring the darned horses," Chester added flatly.

"Wait up now, cowboy," laughed Earl, affably, ignoring Harold's unique bird imitation.

He walked over, took Harold's arm and led him to the other side of the horse.

"You got a better chance if you start from over here."

"Oh, sure," said Harold.

He ducked his head, hoping the big straw hat would hide his crumbling and less than hard-eyed expression. Alternating currents of humiliation and panic cut through him. He wished he had stayed safe in Palm Springs. Then he remembered his grandfather and his aunt's angry words. Not Palm Springs. That wasn't safe either. No, what he really wished is that he'd stayed in LA, but that wasn't possible. He looked up at the vast expanse of the horse's twitching flanks. Surely that wasn't possible either. His stomach heaved, but he managed not to fart again. A small victory. He figured under the circumstances, maybe a large victory.

Earl stood beside him. He patted the horse's leg and muttered something. Then he turned to Harold.

"Don't worry, Harold," he said, low and confidential. "Don't mind them others. Come on, let's get you up. OK, put that left one in here."

He guided Harold's foot into the stirrup.

"Now, just sorta hop on your right and swing it up and over, and... right, you're up there. Easy?"

"Yeah," Harold said, relieved for the moment to be safely in the saddle.

He held on to the pommel, not knowing what to do next.

Earl adjusted his stirrups, pulled the reins over the horse's head and gave them to Harold.

"Now you just relax, Harold. This here is a dude horse, used to kids and such. Ain't that right, Chester?"

Garf and Earl got on their horses, and they all began to ride slowly around the corral. Earl rode next to Harold telling him how to sit, where to put his feet, how to hold the reins. At first he was stiff and unsure, scared about making another mistake and being thrown off. But after ten minutes or so he began to enjoy it. The bulk and power of the horse under him felt good. He liked the view. It was as if he were suddenly four feet taller. And, best of all he wasn't frightened. Not in the least. That surprised him. It isn't so difficult, he said to himself, I can actually do it. Damn if I can't!

"Don't fight it, you just go with it, Harold," Earl cautioned as they began to trot. "It's like being part of the horse. You stay loose and stay right with it. Let your body sorta flow. That's it, flow right along just like you're doing."

It took him a few minutes to find the flow in the midst of the bouncing jolt of the horse's trot, but in the end he did, getting just the right pressure with his legs against the horse's side, the right weight on the stirrups, letting his body rise and fall slightly in time to the rhythm of the horse's movement. When they cantered it was even better. He felt so right, so exhilarated that he had to stop himself from shouting out.

After half an hour they stopped. Still sitting on the horses, Earl rested his hand on Harold's thigh and looked at him questioningly.

"You sure you ain't never been on a horse before, partner?"

"Only when I was little, about six or something like that."

"Well, I'll be damned. You sure didn't start off too good, but I think we got us a natural cowboy here. Wadda you think, Garf?"

"Damn straight! *Viva el vaquero Colorado Grande*!"

Harold grinned. So what if he had a Mexican nickname. It sounded sorta neat anyway, he decided. For the first time since he had been in Palm Springs, Harold felt he had achieved some kind of balance. He realized that he hadn't minded Earl touching him on the leg. Even Aunt Enid's re-designed hat seemed OK.

* * *

Harold's room was empty. He was nowhere in the house. Enid was perplexed. It wasn't like him to wander off without saying anything. In fact, it wasn't like him to leave the house at all. She glanced out into the backyard. The old man was bent over slowly tying his shoelaces.

In the end it had been easier than she had imagined. Once she said it, had told him no, he backed off. Now she just had to stay calm until he left. Say as little as possible. The old bastard had gone down fighting, but seemed to have accepted defeat more or less gracefully. Enid had taken some punches, however, including the last low blow he threw before going down. A well-timed combination. Guilt and anger, anger and guilt. She had braced herself and had ridden it out pretty well. Now there was Harold to worry about.

Where the hell was he? Had he run off because of what she said the night before? In her frustration she had momentarily forgotten that his inert unresponsiveness was a sign of vulnerability not disinterest and that despite his size he was still just a kid. The accident, the deaths, the new surroundings. It would be tough for anyone, even if they weren't going through adolescence. She felt terrible. Poor Harold. When he came back she would have a talk with him, explain about her father and why she had been so upset. She lit a cigarette.

The phone rang. She picked up the receiver, expecting to hear her nephew on the other end. Instead there was a loud hissing and clicking, a gabbled overlay of voices.

"Hello, yes!" she called. "Hello!"

"Enid?" a voice was shouting trying to break through the static. "Enid, can you hear me?"

"Yes, I'm here. Archie?"

"I can hardly hear you, babe. Listen... changes..."

Archie's voice was sucked back into the pool of static.

"Archie? Archie?"

"...after tomorrow. Got that?"

"What, I couldn't hear. The day after tomorrow?"

"I'll be there... call from LA ... give..."

The voice faded away completely. There was a click, the line went dead.

Enid listened to the dial tone for a few seconds before putting down the receiver. She crushed out the cigarette, grinding it absentmindedly over and over again into the glass ashtray. The hot ash burned her fingers. She didn't notice.

So that was that. Two days and he would be there. At least her father would be out of the way by then and she would have only Harold to explain. Sure, only Harold to explain, she thought, smiling to herself. A piece of cake. Archie was going to love it.

"You think this is bad," she would say. "Well, let me tell you what a fortunate guy you are, Archie Blatt."

She tapped her teeth with the ends of her fingernails picturing the scene. It wasn't a nice picture. It was also out of focus. That was because in seven years Enid and Archie had not had a serious fight. A few minor disagreements about where to eat or what movie to go to, but that was it. They had never shown their fangs to each other. Maybe, thought Enid, it was that they were never together for more than a couple of weeks at a time or maybe because they were wary of each other, scared to upset what for both of them was a cozy arrangement. *Was*, thought Enid. Two more days and maybe I'm out on the street again. Me and Harold and a lousy 700 bucks.

And, where the hell was Harold? What if he really had run away? If he didn't come back until after Archie arrived? That would be even worse than his being here. Not only is he living with her in Palm Springs, Archie would think, but he's a problem kid as well. He throws tantrums, runs away from home.

She rushed into Harold's room. The records were still there and, as far as she could tell, all his clothes. The bed hadn't been slept in, though. Could he have left last night? Where would he have gone? He didn't know anyone in Palm Springs except the kid from the stables. She'd have to go down there and ask.

Out by the pool her father was still sitting, staring at the water. She slid open the door.

"I'm just going down the road for a couple of minutes. Will you wait here till I get back?"

He swung his body around in the chair.

"Do you think I could have maybe another cup of coffee?"

Why the stupid maybe, thought Enid? Why not just, "Do you

think I could have another cup of coffee?" The old bastard's still in there trying. She would have to sort it out later. Harold's whereabouts were a more immediate problem.

"Help yourself," she said. "It's on the stove. And close the door when you come in. I don't want the house full of bugs."

"Sure, Enid honey. Don't you worry about a thing."

* * *

"Casey Tibbs? Who's Casey Tibbs?"

"Come on, Harold, ol' son, you ain't gonna sit there and tell me you don't know who Casey Tibbs is?"

"Honest, Earl," said Harold, "I never heard of him."

On the way back from Pioneertown they had stopped for lunch in Yucca Valley. **AL AND BETTY'S PLACE**. An old railway wagon beached on the side of the road. A clapboard building tacked on at the back served as a kitchen. Betty, pinched-faced and fifty, stood behind the formica counter, looking vaguely out at the empty highway through the row of dirty windows. Besides the three boys there was only one other customer, a bony-shouldered man in a black coat, long white hair sticking out from under a flat-brimmed hat. He sat at the far end of the counter, head down, concentrating on his coffee.

"World Champion Cowboy, is all," Garf said indignantly. "Don't they learn you anything at school?"

"Mission Ridge, South Dakota," added Earl, reflectively.

He cupped his hands to his mouth.

"Now coming outta chute number 4 on Billy Boy. Hailing from Mission Ridge, South Dakota!"

Garf took up the announcement

"1949, World Saddle Bronc Cham-pee-on!"

"1951, 1952, 1953 and 1954 World Saddle Bronc Cham-pee-on!" Earl continued.

"1955 All 'round World Ro-deo Cham-pee-on!"

Garf put his arm around Earl's shoulders and they shouted in unison.

"K. C. TIBBS!"

Betty glared at them, her mouth pursed in wrinkled disapproval.

"You boys wanna hold it down?" she scolded, "We got us other people here, you know. Don't wanna have all that carry-on! Now hush-up!"

Earl and Garf shifted uneasily on their stools, trying not to look at each other, trying not to laugh. Harold ducked down behind his hamburger. He wished his new friends were less conspicuous.

"Sorry, ma'am," said Earl.

"It's no bother, Betty, leave 'em be."

The man at the counter stood up and came over to the boys.

"Like the rodeo, do you?" he asked, smiling at them.

Earl nodded.

"From down below?"

"Yes, sir," replied Earl. "Palm Springs."

On hearing the name Palm Springs the man stiffened, threw back his shoulders and seemed to loom up, filling the space in front of them. He waved a thin, accusing finger at Earl.

"Sodom of the Desert! The City of Satan!" he declaimed with passion, his eyes flashing. "Judgment Day is at hand for all those sinners down below who worship Mammon! All those sinners who indulge themselves in Lust, Fornication and Adultery! All those who debauch themselves with strong drink! Mark it well!"

Choking on a wad of half-chewed hamburger, Harold swayed back, away from the unexpected onslaught. It was just like at Alvin's, he thought. On Sundays Alvin and his mother would listen to the radio. He could hear it through the floor. Bible thumpers screaming about Hell and Damnation, about Repenting and Redemption, about the healing power of Christ's merciful love. On and on it went. And all the time Alvin and his mother shouting "Yes, brother!" "Tell it, brother!" "Amen, brother!"

The man leaned down and continued in a softer, more confiding voice.

"Out of the sky it will come down upon them."

He pointed up. The boys' eyes followed the movement. Then he threw his arm straight down.

"And up, up from the bowels of the earth! Fire and ice, boys! Fire and ice!"

"Amen, brother!" responded Betty, her eyes closed, mouth set tight.

"FIRE and ICE!"

That's all I need, thought Harold.

* * *

After having gone about fifty yards, she suddenly realized that she had never walked down the road before. She'd been outside to get the mail and the newspaper, but it hadn't occurred to her actually to go for a walk. In fact, she didn't know anyone in Palm Springs who walked, except on Palm Canyon Drive or on the golf course. Everyone drove. If she went to visit Charlene, who lived only half a mile away, she took the car. Maybe that's why there were no sidewalks, she thought, and as she did she stumbled, her high-heeled slippers catching in the sand by the side of the road. She considered going back to change her shoes, but not wanting to face her father again so soon, she kept moving towards the stables.

It had been difficult to walk on the road in high heels, but it was almost impossible on the soft dirt track inside the stables. She had to watch the ground carefully and take short mincing steps. It was like being on a tightrope, and she put her arms out to her sides so as not to lose her balance.

"You alright, ma'am?" a deep voice boomed.

"Wha..!?" Enid squealed, surprised by the sudden intrusion.

She stopped, wobbling slightly on unsteady legs, and looked up. A very tall man in a cowboy hat, hands on his hips, was standing a few yards in front of her. It was as if he had appeared out of nowhere. She squinted, but the sun was directly behind him and she couldn't see his face. He was completely still, like a colossal statue.

For a few long seconds it was very quiet. She heard herself breathing, felt her heart thumping. She was aware of the smell of horse manure, unfamiliar but unmistakable.

"Ma'am?"

She realized he must have been watching her inelegant struggle across the stable yard. She felt embarrassed and out of place. Not more than a few hundred yards from her own house and in another country. She pulled at the hem of her halter top, suddenly very self-conscious, wishing she had worn something less revealing.

"Excuse me, I'm sorry to bother you, but I live just up the road here, and I'm looking for my nephew, Harold, Harold Abelstein."

"It's no bother, ma'am," said the figure.

She put her hand up to shade her eyes. The man hadn't moved and hadn't answered her question. But then again, she realized that she hadn't actually asked him a direct question.

"Have you seen him? Harold that is."

"Can't rightly say. What does he look like?"

"Yeah, I see, of course, yes, how silly. Well, let's see, he's tallish, sort of heavy-set, red hair. About sixteen years old."

"Nope. Sorry."

"You see, I know he's friendly with a boy who works here."

"That'll be Little Earl."

"That's right, he said his name was Earl. I remember now. Maybe if I could speak to him?"

"Gone."

"Gone?"

"Yep."

It was very hot in the sun and Enid was getting increasingly flustered and frustrated. The man was hoarding his words.

"I see. When do you expect him back."

"Can't rightly say."

This is too much, she thought. Too goddamned much! First that old man who says he's my father running off at the mouth like there's no tomorrow and now this half-assed jerk I can't even see giving me monosyllabic Gary Cooper.

"Listen, you ... you," she exploded, taking a reckless step toward the still figure,"will you stop with this 'Yep-Nope' crap and give me a straight answer to something? He's lost and I've got to find him! God damn it to hell! I've got to!"

She staggered forward in the soft ground, felt her ankle give. She started to fall. A hard hand grabbed her arm. She tried to shake it off, but couldn't.

"Just ease up a tad now, ma'am."

"You let go of me!"

The grip loosened. The man was standing next to her. Now she could see his face. A desert face. Flat cheeks weathered hard, deep set blue eyes, and thin lips, the bottom one blistered by the sun. He smiled at her, not showing his teeth.

"Sorry if I riled you, ma'am," he said, gently letting go of her arm, "but I really ain't seen your boy, and Little Earl, well he went off first thing. Didn't see him."

She felt the sun, too hot on her face. She closed her eyes. Should have worn my hat, she thought. Never go out in summer without a hat. Told Harold. Gave him one as well. Never brought it back though. The hell with this man anyway. Making a fool of me. Myself. Making a fool of myself. Smells awful here. Awful. Got to get away. Ankle hurts. Jesus! Old man's sitting there spitting in my bushes, drinking my coffee. Making himself at home. Harold playing his records, watching television. Making himself at home. Just so he can run away. And Archie. Archie on the way. Sitting in the plane expecting. Always expecting. Paying for it and expecting it.

Enid took a few deep breaths and tried to compose herself. She didn't want to cry there in the stables, in front of someone she didn't know.

"Yes... Thank you," she said finally, turning away so he wouldn't see her face. "Sorry. Sorry to have troubled you. Excuse me."

She took a step.

"Oh shit!" she yelled, as a sharp pain burned through her ankle.

The pain blotted out everything else. She was glad for that.

* * *

He was Earl's father, Big Earl. He ran the riding stables. He smelled strongly of sweat and faintly of horses. They drove back in his pickup to her house.

"You don't want to be worrying yourself too much about the boy," he said, trying to comfort her. "Might be he went with Little Earl after all."

That didn't dispel her worries. Harold wasn't exactly a missing person yet, but how long did she have to wait before he was? And then what?

She leaned heavily on him as he helped her into the house. One breast pressed hard against his arm. She sensed that he felt it. He looked down at her and she could feel his eyes on her body. Men often stared at her. Sometimes she enjoyed it, mostly she didn't. At that moment she didn't.

"You wear them clothes," said Charlene, "with those big ol' tits hanging out like that, wadda you expect. You're just asking for it, honey."

"I don't know," said Enid, "You want to have to walk around in this weather all covered up like some nun or something?"

"I guess not," replied Charlene, "but there's clothes and then there's clothes, if you know what I mean."

"Maybe so, but I dress for me, not for them, damn it!"

"You kidding, Enid honey? Shit! You think they care about that? Hell no they don't. Pigs to the trough!"

"You got something to wrap that with?" he asked after she lowered herself into a chair.

"I think there's an Ace bandage in the medicine cabinet. But, don't..."

"It's all right, ma'am, you shouldn't put any weight on that ankle. Down this way is it?"

She didn't want him in her bathroom, but he was already moving towards the hall. A few moments later he emerged, a small cardboard box in his hand.

"Here we are. How does it feel?"

"It'll be alright, thanks."

She wished he would go so she could be alone with the pain and out from under his disconcertingly direct gaze.

"Mind if I have a look?" he said, kneeling down next to her.

She did, but before she could reply he had cradled her ankle expertly in his hands. He turned it slightly, first one way then the other. She winced.

"That hurt?"

"A little, yeah."

"Don't look too bad, though. Not much swelling. Probably just twisted a tendon, is all."

"How come you know so much about it?"

"Watching the vet working on the horses."

"Thanks a whole lot!" she laughed.

"Oh, no offense meant, ma'am," he said, embarrassed.

"Enid."

He stood up, took off his hat. An inch of white skin ran across the top of his forehead. He seemed to be at a loss what to do next.

"Sure thing, Enid... Well, I gotta be getting back. You be alright?"

"Fine," she said, "and thanks for bringing me home."

"You want me to wrap that for you?"

"No. Thank you very much. I'll take care of it."

He stood staring down at her for a minute or so. He seemed to be on the verge of saying something, but it never came. Then, nodding and hat in hand, he began backing slowly out of the room.

She heard him call to her from the kitchen.

"Good-bye now. You take care."

The screen door banged shut.

Goodnight Irene, Goodnight

She found him lying on his back by the side of the pool behind the palm tree. His arms were splayed out. He was waxen-faced and very still.

Oh my God, she thought, he's dead!

Suspended for a moment, she stood over him staring down. Then as if she were watching from the patio door she saw herself standing over him staring down. The displaced double vision faded, and she heard flies buzzing and the chu-chu-chu sound of a rainbird sprinkler from next door.

I can't believe it, Enid said to herself. The old bastard's died on me! She didn't want him to die by her swimming pool. If he did he would always be there. Back with the family. Every time she went for a swim she would see him. It wasn't fair. Immediately she felt guilty. He was her father.

Fighting to ignore the overpowering stench of sun-ripe body odor and urine, she got down on her knees and lifted his head. He groaned. His eyes fluttered open. Not dead. Not yet. She sighed with relief. That feeling lasted for the three seconds it took the next thought to form.

Dying? God almighty! Even worse than dead! Days or weeks he could linger. He would only have to last for two days. It wouldn't matter after that, Archie would be there. What could she possibly say to him?

"Archie I'm sorry but my father, who I'm sure you can smell. Yes? Well he's just in the process of dying in my dressing room there across the hall. Hear that? No, it's only his cough. Oh yes, and I forgot to mention, you know that enormous redheaded kid watching television and playing loud music in the living room? My nephew, Harold. That's right, he's sleeping on the couch. Won't bother us at all."

Another wave of guilt rolled in. He was her father. Maybe her dying father. And her sister's son, her dead sister's son, her dead sister's missing son.

She pushed her hair out of her eyes and looked at the man she was holding. He didn't seem to have any weight. If she let go of him he might be blown away like an empty paper bag, end over end until he caught up against a fence or went into the swimming pool.

"What happened!?" she asked, urgently.

"Happened?" he replied. "Who... Oh, it's you."

He opened his mouth to speak. It was as if a sewer had burst She jerked her head away from the smell.

With her face averted, she propped him up against the palm tree. He was perspiring and cold to the touch. There was dried blood on his shirt. A coffee cup lay broken on the edge of the pool.

"Just rest there," she said. "I'll call a doctor."

"Don't need a doctor!" he said, with surprising passion. "Don't... be alright ... in a minute. Just give... me a minute."

He tried to stand up, but could only get as far as his knees. He held onto the palm tree, mouth agape, breathing hard.

"Just... another... minute," he said, punctuating each word with a gasp.

"What happened?" she insisted. "What's the matter?"

He sat down again heavily, legs straight out in front of him. His eyes were glazed. He swallowed with difficulty and then began to talk, all the time staring fixedly at the swimming pool, his hands clawing weakly at different parts of his body — arms, leg, chest.

"You know how old he was when he died?" Abe asked weakly. "Huh? Do you? No? Forty-seven. That's all. Forty-seven years old he was. Had years left in him. Years and years."

"What are..." Enid began.

He ignored her, continuing to talk and scratch.

"A man of old he was. A knight in shining armor. The sword of truth. God and country. Great American patriot. Wouldn't let them hide anywhere. Huh? No he would not. Nowhere to hide from old Joe. It didn't..."

He started to cough from deep in the chest. His body shook as he fought to suck in enough air. It took him a few minutes to recover.

"You don't have a smoke, do you?"

"Listen," Enid admonished, "you're..."

He wasn't listening.

"And, she... the wife... only thirty-one... thirty-one. Catholics. It didn't matter,' he said, his voice trailing off. 'Nothing matters now."

Clearing his throat, he brought up a lump of phlegm, arched his neck and tried to spit it into the pool. He didn't have the strength. It landed on his pants leg. They both watched transfixed as the yellow glob changed shape, flowed downwards to form a heavy tadpole-like head and then, detaching itself, fell to the ground between his legs.

Enid felt sick to her stomach. He's gone, she thought. Snapped. I've got to get him out of here. Into a hospital or something. But out of my house. Out before Archie arrives.

Abe Cohen smiled to himself and fell silent. He stared at his hands as if they belonged to someone else.

As she watched him, intermittent reflections from the pool shimmered across the old man's thin face giving him an air of dramatic nobility. A fallen warrior. A defeated chieftain dying by the water's edge.

"Balls to that!"said Enid vehemently.

She stood up and limped back towards the house.

* * *

"It's not that we *won't* take him to the hospital, Miss Carlson, it's just that I don't think there is any point in doing so at this stage."

The doctor wore canary-yellow pants and a shirt covered in large blue parrots. He was new to Palm Springs. He had just come from the golf course.

"Stage? Stage of what?"

He searched her face.

"You don't know, do you?" he sighed.

"Know what?"

As she said it she knew but she didn't want to know any more than that.

The doctor hesitated, tapping the end of his stethoscope against his hand. She wished old Plumstead wasn't on vacation; she could talk to him. This one seemed so young, younger than her, probably just out of medical school. He wouldn't understand that she wasn't responsible. That she couldn't be responsible.

"You said he was your father?"

"Yes, that's right, but..."

"Has Dr. Plumstead treated him before?"

"No. No, he hasn't, but listen to me, please. I know I said he's my father, but he arrived only last night. He doesn't live here, you see."

"Yes. Ah, well then... Miss Carlson, would you like to sit down for a minute?"

She sat down. The doctor perched on the side of the dining room table. He looked up at the ceiling, reluctant to begin.

"Well?" she said.

"I'm afraid it's bad news, Miss Carlson. Very bad news, in fact. You see, your father is suffering from extremely advanced ureamia. That's caused by renal — what you would know as kidney — failure. He also has a serious lung problem. Emphysema, if I'm not mistaken."

He waited for a response. When none came he continued.

"Ordinarily, I would have to have some blood tests done in order to confirm the diagnosis on the kidneys, but in this case it really isn't necessary."

"Not necessary? Why not?" she asked indignantly. "If he went into the hospital you could do the tests there, couldn't you? You could call an ambulance right now and..."

"I'm trying to explain that to you. Your father tells me that he recently discharged himself from Memorial Hospital in Los Angeles."

"How could he discharge... I thought with emphysema..."

"That's not the main difficulty here," the doctor interrupted. "It's the kidneys I'm afraid. And there's nothing whatsoever we can do about that. They've virtually stopped working. Once that happens it's only a matter of time... I'm terribly sorry."

Enid fumbled in her pockets for a cigarette. Her fingers were numb. She managed to put a cigarette in her mouth but didn't light it.

"Time? How much time?"

"Hard to say. In cases like this it could be a day, two days. If he's lucky maybe a week."

Lucky, she thought. If *he's* lucky!

"Isn't there something...?"

The doctor shook his head.

"Nothing. We simply don't have a treatment. He'll just sort of slip away. But, at least you can be thankful that there won't be much pain. I can give you some pills and..."

"Wait! Wait just a minute, please," Enid said, desperate to explain. "You don't understand, I told you before, he doesn't live here with me. He *never* has lived here. I haven't seen him for twenty-five years. Twenty-five years! You can't expect..."

Her voice trailed off. She didn't want this to be happening. Didn't believe it was happening. Only an hour ago everything was fine. She'd told him to go. He was on his way. One more cup of coffee and gone. She would be out from under. Now he was lying in her — that is in Harold's room. Lying in there stinking to high heaven and dying. And he would linger, she knew the son of a bitch would linger. Stink and linger. Linger and stink. She stubbed out the unlit cigarette and took another one.

"I do understand, Miss Carlson how you feel, but..."

She leapt from the chair. Throwing her arms up in frustration and despair and ignoring her painful ankle she advanced on the doctor.

"Miss Carlson, please," he said, retreating towards the kitchen.

"Do you? Do you understand? You don't understand anything! I can't have him here! I won't have him here! I..."

She stopped, suddenly distracted, turned away from the doctor and wandered over to the picture window. Something he said had just then clicked into place.

Wait a minute, she thought. Wait. He discharged himself from the hospital? Then he knew. He must have known he was dying. He never had any intention of leaving. He wants to die here with me. All that song and dance about laying over a few days was so much crap. The scheming bastard!

While her back was turned the doctor hastily wrote out a prescription and put it on the table. He closed his bag and started for the door.

"He should be alright for a while," he called out. "I gave him something to make him sleep. I'll come by tomorrow. In the meantime if you need anything else, or if there is a sudden change in his condition don't hesitate to call."

"You're going?" she asked, snapping out of her daydream.

She limped over and latched on to his arm. The doctor squirmed, tried to free himself but couldn't. Enid's fingers dug into him. Her urgency pulled him off balance and he fought not to topple over.

"Please, Miss Carlson, I know you're upset, but please..."

"You can't go just like this! What am I supposed to do? I can't take care of him. I don't want him here. Don't want him dying here in my house. You've got to take him with you, doctor. Got to! I've got someone coming. I've..."

"It's not that simple, Miss Carlson. Ah, please my arm."

Enid stared at him. He didn't meet her eyes. Finally she relaxed her grip. He gently lifted his arm away from her still-clenched hand and stepped back towards the door.

"You must understand," he said, adopting a more formal, doctorly tone. "We cannot admit people to the hospital simply because they are inconvenient. Can you imagine what that would mean? Besides, he doesn't want to go into the hospital. He told me so himself."

"He doesn't want?" Enid shouted. "He doesn't want? What about me? Huh? What about what I want? Isn't that important?"

"Miss Carlson!" he said with as much disdainful authority as he could muster. "For pity sake, when all is said and done he is your father! Let the man at least die with some dignity in the bosom of his family."

Enid slumped against the wall, defeated. She saw herself, heard her own voice and felt ashamed. She realized that she had been making a fool of herself. Another silly, hysterical woman. A selfish, heartless monster. Of course. She wanted to throw her dying father out into the street didn't she? Of course, silly, hysterical. Of course, a heartless monster. If she could only explain it all to him. Tell him about her mother, about the terrible struggle they had, about herself having to grow up without a father, but how, she thought with a resigned smile, can you explain anything to a man who wears yellow pants and a shirt covered with blue parrots.

In any case he was right, wasn't he? Abe Cohen was her father and he was dying. That was just the way it was.

* * *

"You shitting me, Harold?"

"No, I'm serious, Earl. Why not?"

"Well, hell, boy, that's just nigger music, that's all it is."

"Yeah," Garf chimed in, "nigger music."

It made Harold uncomfortable when anyone said nigger. He heard it all the time at school. That and *shvartzeh.* "You can't trust the *shvartzehs.*" "You're as lazy as a *shvartzeh.*" On and on. Harold didn't understand why the kids at Fairfax seemed to dislike Negroes so much. Probably because they didn't know any better, just like Earl and Garf.

"I just like it, that's all," Harold said, defensively, wanting to end the conversation.

He decided it would be a waste of time trying to explain to Earl and Garf about Alvin Harper, about why he liked rhythm and blues, why he collected records and why the detailed knowledge was so important to him. What could you explain to a couple of dumb-ass-ignorant Palm Springs cowboys? Anyway, he wasn't sure he could explain it to himself.

He looked away into the desert. Lots of white sand and scraggy bushes. It all looked the same to him. His grandfather had been right. Empty and far away from anywhere.

They were driving through the Pass on their way back to Palm Springs. On the radio Jim Reeves was singing something about bright lights and moths. The pickup rolled and bucked in the strong cross wind. Wanting to appear at ease, Harold leaned his arm on the open window. He swallowed a shout of pain as the metal frame burned into his soft flesh and the furnace-hot wind seared his elbow. Quickly he pulled his arm inside, hoping the others wouldn't notice. They didn't.

"What about country music?" asked Earl. " Hank Williams? Bill Monroe? Earnest Tubb? Roy Acuff? Or Jim Reeves?"

He pointed to the radio.

"I bet you never even listened to the Grand Ole Opry."

"Um... not really," Harold replied uneasily, rubbing his scorched arm.

"City boy," laughed Garf.

Harold's recent success at Pioneertown seemed to be fading fast.

* * *

"Where the *hell* have you been?"

Aunt Enid, hands on hips, stood in front of the house. Harold had never seen her so angry. It was worse than the night by the pool. Now the anger was clearly directed at him. More echoes of his mother.

Gingerly, he climbed down from the pickup. The insides of his thighs ached and the burn on his arm was stinging. He knew that behind him Earl and Garf were listening and watching.

"I've been worried sick about you, Harold," his aunt scolded. "Do you know what time it is? Do you? I was just about to call the police."

Even his mother had never gone that far.

"You take care now, Harold," called Earl from the pickup. "And watch out for Big Jim."

Harold turned around. Both boys were grinning broadly at him. He felt humiliated and completely alone. Head hanging he followed his aunt into the house. He heard Earl's pickup accelerate down the road.

When they got inside she began to shout at him once more.

"You must never, I repeat never do that again, Harold! Never go off without telling me... You can't imagine how I..."

Then throwing her arms around him she began to weep. She hugged him tightly.

"I'm so happy Harold... You've come... so worried."

Harold stood there, his arms dangling at his sides, not knowing what to do. Yelling he could handle. For him being yelled at was normal and he had had lots of practice ignoring it. Crying and hugging were altogether different, especially from Aunt Enid. There was no way to ignore, no room to ignore. He felt her breasts squishing against his chest, felt the tears soaking through his shirt.

He was mortified by the physical intimacy, terrified by the tears. After a minute or two she let go and stepped back.

"I'm sorry, Harold darling, but I've had a very, *very* bad day. And when I didn't find you this morning I thought... Well, it doesn't matter now. You're home. That's the most important thing, isn't it?"

Then she noticed the hat he was wearing.

"Why Harold," she laughed, "what have you done to my hat?"

"Uh... I didn't. It was Earl, Garf really. You see he, that is they, thought that..."

Harold's voice trailed off. Mystified, Enid watched her nephew fading away in front of her.

It's just like the *500 Hats of Bartholomew Cubbins*, Harold thought dreamily. "Well," demanded the king again,"do you or do you not take off your hat before your king?" When he was a little kid it had been his favorite story. Every night he asked his parents to read it to him. Every night they argued about whose turn it was to read to him. Finally they bought a recording of the book. Four shiny black 78s. Much better than his parents, he had decided. There were trumpets and different voices, the sounds of a carriage racing over cobbled streets, of the axeman's axe hitting the execution block and best of all, he didn't have to rely on his parents. He could listen to the story any time and as many times as he wanted. He wondered whatever happened to those records.

"Are you alright, darling?" asked Enid, approaching him and gently touching his arm.

The contact brought him out of his reverie and back to where he was. More importantly, it brought him back to where his aunt was, which was much too close.

"Sure, yes, Aunt Enid. Fine," he said, sliding around her and making for the sanctuary of his room.

"Harold, please dear, we must talk right this minute. Something very serious has come up."

She had been too busy to worry about how to tell Harold that his room was now occupied by her dying father. She looked at him and hesitated. Eyes averted, shoulders slumped, patches of blistered skin still marking his face, her nephew stood solidly in front of her. He reeked of horses.

"Can we sit down, Harold?"

They sat down. She reached across the table and took his hand. It was soft, moist and ungiving. Just like Harold, she thought sadly.

Not that it was any easier to deal with, but he was getting used to bad news. He stared down at his feet waiting for the latest installment. After she told him whatever it was at least then he would be able to get away from her and bury himself in the controllable certainty of his records.

She told him.

* * *

They had washed him, but the smell of urine still hung in the air.

"You're a good boy, Harold. A very good boy."

Abe Cohen was lying in bed covered with a thin blanket, but Harold couldn't erase the picture of the old man's naked body from his mind.

"I don't care what the doctor says," Aunt Enid had said, "I'm not having him in here smelling like this. But I can't do it by myself, Harold. You will simply have to help me. OK?"

They had carried him, half comatose, into the bathroom and set him down on the floor near the bathtub. He slumped there, eyes closed, arms and legs limp, moaning softly.

"You hold him upright," Enid said, "and I'll try to get these clothes off him."

The stench coming from the old man was stomach turning. Harold imagined he could detect the smell of decaying flesh under the stronger smells of piss and BO. His stomach heaved, threatening to bring up his lunch. He fought to keep it down.

"I don't know about this, Aunt Enid," Harold said faintly. "I don't feel so good."

"Harold," she said sternly, "I don't feel so great either and he feels a lot worse. I'm depending on you now. Please!"

She bent over and began unbuttoning her father's shirt. Sweat beaded her forehead and ran down the side of her face. She was inches away from him and Harold couldn't stop himself staring down the front of her halter top. Every few seconds the dark corner of a nipple would be exposed as her breasts moved back and forth.

Despite the awful smell drifting off his grandfather, he started to get an erection. It all made him very light-headed.

"Don't let him slip!"

Startled by her shout, he pulled his eyes away from her breasts and held his grandfather more firmly. By then she had removed his shirt and was starting on his pants. Harold tried not to look at the body that was emerging. He couldn't help himself.

Chest, arms, and legs were emaciated: sharp bones wrapped in translucent parchment. The stomach hung from between the hips like a bloated sack. The skin over the entire body was mottled and covered in a dusty white rash. The pubic hair had disappeared almost entirely, cruelly exposing the penis and testicles, purplish-brown and shrunken to the size of a child's.

Harold was revolted by the sight and by the feel of the body. It was brittle and lifeless. If he squeezed too hard the bones would snap and a thin colorless fluid would ooze onto the floor.

A caricature of a person, a bad joke. Does this happen to everyone, he wondered, unable to take his eyes off his grandfather's withered genitals. Will it happen to me? His erection had long since evaporated. He knew beyond certainty that he would never have another one.

His grandfather flickered awake when they lowered him into the water.

"Where... Enid? What are you doing?"

He made a feeble effort to resist.

"It's alright, Dad, it's alright," said Enid softly, as if she was calming a baby, "Just relax, you'll feel better in a few minutes."

All turned around, thought Harold. Could he have done this for his father? It didn't seem possible. How could Aunt Enid do it? Especially since she seemed to hate him so much. Yet there she had been, on her knees, bathing her father. He didn't understand.

From the bed Abe's cocked finger now reeled in Harold's reluctant attention.

"How old are you, Harold?"

"Sixteen. I told you that before."

"Right, you did. I'm sorry, of course, sixteen years old. A good age to be. Better than sixty-five. You hear what I'm saying? A lot better."

Abe paused and gazed at the walls, as if seeing them for the first time.

"You like roses?"

Harold smiled.

"Not much."

"Never did like them myself," said Abe. "Don't know why. And here I am stuck in a room full of roses. It's a funny life. A funny life. Now daisies, daisies are a different story. I've always liked daisies."

Eyes turned inward, he began to hum.

"You know that one, Harold?"

Harold shook his head.

In a soft and slightly off-key voice Abe sang, "Day-z Day-z give me your answer do. I'm half cray-z all for the love of you. It won't be a stylish marriage, I can't afford a carriage, but you'd look sweet upon the seat of a bicycle built for two."

"My mother..." Abe said, rubbing his eyes.

His head fell back on the pillow, and his eyes closed. Thinking the old man had dozed off again, Harold got up from the bed. Abe's voice caught him before he got halfway across the room.

"You like the fights, Harold?"

He didn't wait for a reply.

"How about that Sugar Ray? Huh? Stopping Fulmer in the fifth with that left hook. So sweet. Bang! Right on the chin. Never knew what hit him. On his way back to Utah. A puncher and a mover. Thirty-six years old, Harold. Thirty-six years old and still the best. You hear what I'm saying? Still the best. But, this Patterson guy, I can't see him lasting, can you? Too small for a real heavyweight and he doesn't box right. Peek-a-boo! Peek-a-boo. What is that? More like chick-en-shit. You hear what I'm saying? You watch what Hurricane Jackson does to him in the rematch."

Harold didn't know a thing about boxing. His mother hadn't allowed his father watch the fights on their television.

"I got better things to do than watch a couple of poor *shvartzehs* beating each other to death. And so do you, Norman. Besides I don't want Harold watching such things."

"I'm going out, Sylvia."

"That's right, you go to Murry's. Go on. Watch the fight, have some drinks with the boys. You're pathetic, Norman! You hear me? Pathetic!"

He could still hear the door slam.

"What about those Dodgers and Giants, Harold?" Abe asked, trying another tack to get the boy's attention. "What do you think about that, huh?"

"Oh, they're OK, I guess."

"You guess? But, what about them coming out here to the West Coast? Really something isn't it? I don't see how it's going to work, though. The nearest team, the Cardinals, two thousand miles away in St. Louis. Two thousand miles. And in New York they're going nuts. Can you imagine Brooklyn without the Dodgers? Without Ebbet's Field, for God sake? Can you? No, it'll never work. You hear what I'm saying? Never work."

Once, after a lot of pleading, his father had taken him to Gilmore Field to see the Angels play. But all the time they were there he was talking the game down. His father was from the East, a Dodgers fan.

"Sure Bilko can hit homers here. Anyone can in a little rinky-dink park like this, Harold. Look at that play, will you! Bush league stuff. Not the real thing. Not the majors. You see a Duke Snider here? Or a Sandy Amoros? A Don Drysdale? Of course you don't."

It was the only sporting event he had ever been to with his father. They never went to another one. At the time it hadn't seemed so important.

"She's a good woman, your aunt. Hey, you listening to me?"

Harold hadn't been.

"Sure," he said, "Aunt Enid."

"Yeah, a good woman at heart. Taking me in like this. Taking *you* in for that matter."

That was just what Harold did not want to hear. The old man and he were separate, not a package deal. He remembered the look on Aunt Enid's face that night by the pool. His grandfather's being there had already messed things up for him. Aunt Enid was preoccupied and nervy and he had lost his room. The one place, despite the roses, where he had felt comfortable. All his records and his record player were now in the garage, his clothes in the closet by the front door, and a stranger was dying in his bed.

Maybe he could go down to the stables tomorrow. He would tell Aunt Enid this time. It would be OK if Garf wasn't there, if he could just be with Earl. Maybe he'd let him ride again.

"You know how she makes a living, your aunt? I mean, what is it, Wednesday? Tuesday? What?"

"Wednesday."

"Wednesday, right. And, she hasn't gone to work, has she? And, she's not married. So?"

"So?"

"So, where does she get her money?"

He knew. Of course he did. She had told him about the man from St. Louis. But he was not going to tell his grandfather. It wasn't any of his business and, besides, he didn't want him to know too much about Aunt Enid. That would put them on a more even footing. Also, he felt somehow that he should protect his aunt from her father. Harold had seen the pain on her face and the tears when she was bathing him. He didn't want her to be vulnerable like that. It made him feel insecure.

"She's got a nice house here. A nice car. Nice furniture. It all grew from a tree, did it?"

"I dunno," Harold replied.

* * *

"So what was I supposed to do? I ask you. What? I didn't want to die there among strangers."

"You could have at least told me when you arrived," Enid said, trying to keep the annoyance out of her voice.

He is my father. He is dying.

She repeated the litany to herself. Over and over.

"I should have said? Maybe. OK. Maybe I should have. I'm sorry. It's just that, you know it's hard. Hard to say that to someone. 'Hello, I'm your father and I'm dying.' You hear what I'm saying, Enid?"

In spite of herself, she smiled.

"Loud and clear."

"How about, 'Loud and clear, Dad'? I'm a non-person? I don't have a name all of a sudden?"

Goodnight Irene, Goodnight

One moment of weakness when he was lying helpless in the bath. A sudden rush of pity and there he was at her with guilt. She didn't answer.

"OK. I understand. Sure, why not? Don't worry about it though. ... It's just that with such little time left it would have been nice. But I shouldn't expect. I know I shouldn't expect."

He is my father. He is dying.

"Who's Daddy's little girl? Daddy's sweetness?"

Sitting on his lap, strong arms holding her close. Dark furniture, a framed oval mirror on the opposite wall, outside the metal lattice of the fire escape, the dull rumble from the street five floors below. White lace doilies on the back of the couch, on the arms of the overstuffed chairs. Tobacco and frying onions. Her mother calling out from the kitchen.

Resting on the white pillow his head seemed much smaller, as if it were there all by itself, not connected to the blanket-hidden body.

"I have so much to tell you," Abe said, straining to sit up, "but I feel so damn tired... It's funny, you know, dying that is. At first, when they told me in Los Angeles about the kidneys, I didn't feel anything. The truth, I didn't."

He held up his right hand as if he were taking an oath.

"Nothing. I didn't believe. I mean really believe it. Later when I did I was scared. Frozen stiff scared. You know what I thought about? A million years and you wouldn't guess. No? I could only think about all the time I'd spent, so much time, sixty-five years, dressing, washing myself, brushing my teeth, having my hair cut, cleaning my ears, all those things I'd done to my body."

He gave a short laugh and then started to cough. The blanket shook and rippled. It took him a few minutes to recover.

"And what did it all amount to? Cleaning, washing, brushing. What? Nothing. In the end a big round nothing."

He wiped his eyes, then lay back staring at the ceiling. His voice became dreamy. The words seemed to float out of his mouth.

"Sometimes I think of that little kid. What was his name? You know the one who fell down that well in New York somewhere. Benny. That's it Benny, Benny Hooper. Remember that? No? They gave him up for dead. Down there twenty-four hours, last rites and everything. Then at the last minute, the walls are collapsing on top of him and they pull him out. Just like that. Pulled and pop, out he came. Yeah, little Benny Hooper. Makes you think. Huh?"

"Sure," she replied flatly, "it makes you think."

She was thinking, but not about Benny Hooper. She was thinking how she had resigned herself to his being there. To his dying there. About how she would go through the motions. Do the right thing. There was nothing else she could do.

Archie? The day after tomorrow, he would step off the plane. Her father might be dead by then. He did seem to be a lot weaker than when he first arrived. She tried to push the thought away. It wouldn't go. She wanted him dead and out of her house, out of her life.

And if not? If he was still hanging on? Surely Archie wouldn't just throw me out into the road, she thought? A dying father and an orphaned nephew. I couldn't like a man who would do that, could I? But, who knows. When the chips are down, they're down. Down to his privacy gone, his desert hideaway overrun. Archie Blatt's woman, his woman no longer. Now Harold Abelstein's aunt, Abe Cohen's daughter.

Archie always made such a lot of noise in bed. How was he going to feel with the old man right across the hall listening and Harold asleep or watching TV in the living room? Not good. Not good at all.

He would be very civil about it, very understanding. Maybe even sympathetic. She was sure of that. No yelling, no immediate drastic moves, but when he got back home he would see things differently. What do I need this for, he would ask himself? For this kind of *tsouris* I could stay in St. Louis, she could hear him say.

First the rent wouldn't be paid. The real estate guy would call up and ask about it. She wouldn't be able to contact Archie. Then the checks would stop coming. Maybe he would change his phone number or tell his secretary that he was out. Archie could do that. He was a businessman. He made those kinds of decisions. And then what?

Abe had closed his eyes. He was asleep.

It was too hot. She stood up and closed the window. Cooler air from the wall vent began to fill the room.

And All They Will Call You Will Be...

"It'll be alright, Harold. A temporary arrangement is all until, until... well you know. Listen, it won't be so bad, you'll have your own room and you can have lunch and dinner here with us. Charlene said to bring your records if you wanted to. It's a nice house and I'm sure you'll get along with John. He loves children. Not to say you're a child, darling. Of course not. But, you know what I mean. I'll take you over after you've had breakfast. OK?"

First he had lost his room and now she was farming him out to Charlene. Horrible, cooing, groping, fat-fingered Charlene and her husband John, who loves children. Complete blackness. A total nightmare.

"Can't I just sorta sleep there?" Harold asked desperately, pointing to the couch. "I won't be in the way, really."

"Well, darling, if it was only me, of course you could. But, there's your grandfather, and tomorrow my friend Archie's flying in from Los Angeles. The house just isn't big enough for all of us right now. You can see that, can't you?"

He could and he couldn't. Besides, it wasn't fair. He'd been there first. Who was this Archie guy, anyway?

"Uh-huh," he said, downcast.

I have to do this, Enid told herself sternly. Have to and that's that. Can't let myself feel guilty. He's young, he'll get over it. It's not like I'm hiding him away from Archie or anything like that. I'm just saving myself unnecessary aggravation, that's all. And, he'll be more comfortable at Charlene's. A room of his own. Better for everyone.

Still, she found it difficult to watch Harold. Eyes blank, mouth sagging, he sat across the table from her, aimlessly running his finger around the rim of a glass. It was half-filled with milk. There was a white high tide mark on his upper lip. It made him seem much younger.

She reached across the table and patted his hand.

"We'll survive this, Harold. You and your Aunt Enid. We'll survive, won't we, darling?"

"Yeah," he said glumly, not looking up, "Is there any Bosco in the kitchen?"

Maybe survive, she thought. On the other hand, maybe not.

On the second front the battle was also not going very well. During the night Abe had fouled the bed. He was weeping when she came into the room.

"Please, don't," she said to him, wanting to cry as well.

She forced herself to ignore the raw smell of shit that overfilled the room and tried to imagine how her father must feel.

He lay there, his head turned away, sobs shaking his body.

"Never happened before... I never... never..." he muttered over and over again.

She had helped him into the bathroom. He seemed to weigh less than the day before. She put him into the bathtub and washed him. He continued to sob, all the while mumbling to himself. After a few minutes he calmed down, accepting her attention. When she had finished he sat unselfconsciously on the toilet with a big towel draped over his shoulders and talked.

"The Sally Army it was. I thought they were all bands, Christ, and that kinda thing. You know what I mean? You might have been married, changed your name. I didn't know. But they found you for me, didn't they?"

Thank you, Salvation Army, thought Enid.

"They even gave me the train fare. Me. Ha! Abe Cohen. They knew I wasn't, you know? How could I be? Didn't matter though."

He stopped talking, gasped for breath. Without moving his body suddenly seemed to fold in on itself.

"Enid, do you think maybe I could go and lie down again for a while?"

* * *

Harold had expected a big man. Someone with the physical bulk to match Charlene's. The only thing big about him was his voice.

"Hi there, Harold!," he boomed, thrusting out a surprisingly delicate hand. "John Briggs. How are you today? Settling in OK?"

"Fine thank you, sir."

"Hey now, none of that sir stuff here. No sir! Ha! Ha! No sir! Can you beat that? Listen to me, willya. It's just plain John. You call me John. OK?"

"Sure, right, John."

"That's the ticket."

He slapped Harold on the back.

"Now you're cooking!" he bellowed.

Short and thin, if you were charitable you might call him dapper. Like a small imprecise copy of Fred Astaire, Harold thought, only more stick insect like. Maybe it was the black pencil-thin moustache.

"You get all your gear stowed away? Everything shipshape?"

"Yes, thanks, uh, Mr., I mean, John."

"Good. Very Good. Well, now," he said, rubbing his hands together briskly and rocking back on the tiny heels of his tiny feet, "Where's the little woman?"

Harold wondered who he was talking about.

Harold and Enid and Abe and Archie

Feeling Tomorrow Like I Feel Today

"Do I have to stay actually in there with him? The smell, and he's not making..."

"Harold, he is your grandfather. He is dying. What else can I tell you?"

"And Earl said I could come down there. That maybe I could..."

"Harold? You want to leave him alone? You want to do that?"

Guilt. Always guilt. His mother had been a master of guilt. A grand master. Especially effective were her questions ending with *for you.*

"I didn't make the egg soft enough *for you*? I should have stood there longer waiting in the sun *for you*? You think I'd be doing this if it wasn't *for you*?"

He had never been able to work out an adequate defense.

"No, Aunt Enid. Sorry."

"I won't be long. Just to the airport and straight back. Twenty minutes at the most. You can hold down the fort for that long, can't you, darling?"

The last time he had seen his aunt so dressed up was at the funeral. Now she wore light colors. A fancy dress, stockings, high heels, a wide-brimmed hat, and a brassiere that lifted up her tits and made them look larger and more pointy. Also lots of make-up. He didn't like it when she looked so exaggerated. Eyes too big, mouth too big, tits too big.

"Good-bye, darling," she said, kissing him on the cheek. "Take care of everything."

The door closed behind her. With the back of his hand he wiped the lipstick off his face.

"Enid," Abe called weakly from the bedroom. "Enid."

Reluctantly, Harold went in to see his grandfather.

"She's gone out for a little while," he explained. "To pick up someone from the airport."

Harold didn't know whether his aunt had told the old man anything about Archie. He wasn't going to. Besides, he didn't know that much himself. A boyfriend from St. Louis who took care of her. Someone he had to be good friends with. That was about it. The whole thing made him uneasy. First the old man and now Archie. What would it mean for him? She did say they would survive, didn't she? He and Aunt Enid. It sounded alright, although he wasn't sure exactly what she meant. It's not that he wanted her attention exactly. In fact, he recoiled from it. But then again he wasn't exactly sure.

His feelings confused him. He didn't like to think about them too much.

He wished he could go down to the stables and hang around with Earl for a while. Then he could at least escape from the old man's stink, which had by then invaded the hallway. Even the Air-Wick couldn't kill it. He could also get away from the probing questions and the incessant rambling monologues.

"Who's she picking up?" asked Abe.

"A friend, I think," Harold answered.

"A friend? Her friend from St. Louis?"

"Dunno," replied Harold.

So, she had told him. But, how much? It didn't matter, Abe had zeroed in on St. Louis and was off in search of something else.

"I knew this guy from St. Louis once. Met him when I was in Chicago in '37. I think it was '37. I suppose it could have been '38. Anyway, did I tell you this one before? No? Well..."

Harold sighed.

The evenings weren't much better. Charlene talked at him as if he were a three-year old, all but tickling him under the chin, and John — she actually called him Big John — told him all about real estate in Palm Springs.

"Bargains! Golden opportunities, Harold! I'm here to tell you. And, this is straight from the horse's mouth. They're selling like hotcakes! Absolute hotcakes! You know, I tell the people when I take them out to see a property, I tell them, 'Listen, it's cheap at twice the price.' If that doesn't do the trick, I say, 'What's the matter, folks, are you saving it all for a rainy day?' And then I spring it on them. 'Well,' I say, 'You can't go wrong, because it never rains in sunny Palm Springs!' Ha! Ha! Doesn't that just take the cake!?"

"Harold? Harold? A glass of water please, Harold?"

The story about the man in St. Louis had ended.

Harold got up, went into the bathroom and filled a glass for his grandfather.

* * *

A telegram had come the night before. No chance to give him a hint, to soften the impact. She would have to explain everything between the airport and the house. That would give her ten minutes at the most. Not nearly enough time.

She looked at her watch. The plane would land in fifteen minutes, at 11:30. I'll take him into the Village first, she thought. Talk to him over lunch. Archie's happy when he's eating.

She started the car, pulled out into the road and headed towards Sunrise. Passing the stables, she saw Earl and his father. They were unloading bales of hay from a big truck. She tooted her horn and waved. They glanced up but didn't wave back. Maybe they don't recognize the car, Enid said to herself.

Archie would want to come straight back to the house. For seven years that had been the ritual. To the house and to bed. He was often so worked up it was all she could do to keep him from starting in the car. In the turmoil of the last few days she had completely forgotten how horny he was when he arrived.

"Hey, you know what, babe? I get this incredible hard-on the minute I walk on the plane. Gee, isn't that something? A guy my age? Have to fly all the way with a copy of *Life* on my lap!"

She'd tell him she was hungry. That there was nothing to eat in the house. Any excuse for a breathing space. Not that it would do any good in the end. She had resigned herself to that, but couldn't think past what it would mean when the money stopped coming. First she had to deal with today.

It suddenly occurred to her that she was selling Archie short. If he really loved her, like he said he did, it all might work out. Why not? Her father was not going to be around much longer. Even Harold. He was sixteen. Going into the eleventh grade in September. A couple of years more and he'd probably be gone. Sure. Why couldn't she sell that to Archie? If he really loved her. No problem. She smiled and drummed her fingers on the steering wheel. Things were not all that bad. Sure. She'd been stupid to get herself so worried and upset.

She pulled up at the stop sign on the corner of Sunrise. There was no one coming. She made a right turn and put her foot down. As she did the smothering doubts rolled in once again. Did he love her? In eight years they had never spent longer than two weeks together at any time. Honeymoons. Three, sometimes four a year. How much could you tell from that? Relaxed, problem-free vacations for Archie. Golf and sex. Sure, he had loved her. What was not to love? It was all exactly what he wanted and how he wanted it. On a platter. She smacked the steering wheel with the palm of her hand. Sure, she thought, on a platter!

What did they talk about? To be more precise, what did he talk about? His work, his sick wife, his horrible kids, his problems. He wasn't inattentive to her problems, she couldn't say that. It was just that they never really talked about them in the same way. His answer was always the same. He bought her things. That was part of the deal. She listened and was sympathetic, he listened and paid. Maybe Sylvia had been right, she thought sadly. A high-class whore. Why high-class even? She had never allowed those thoughts in before. They depressed her.

She turned left onto Amado, a shortcut to the airport. It was 11:25. Shaking a cigarette out of the pack, she put one in her mouth and bent forward to push in the lighter on the dashboard. Just then there was a loud bang and the car lurched violently to the left. Enid hit the brakes and threw all her strength against the steering wheel. The rear wheels locked and the car went into a spin. She was thrown sideways and then forward, hard against the windshield. The car skidded out of control and finally came to a lopsided rest in the soft sand by the side of the road.

* * *

Feeling Tomorrow Like I Feel Today

The end of his tongue sticking out thoughtfully from the corner of his mouth, Harold spread the peanut butter thickly. The bits of peanut that dotted the slice of bread were soon covered by strawberry jam. He slapped on another piece of bread and coated it with mashed banana and another layer of peanut butter. Having finished constructing the triple-decker, he opened the refrigerator and took out a carton of milk. He picked up a glass, carried everything into the dining room and sat down.

For the moment he was content.

His grandfather had fallen asleep and his aunt was still not back from the airport. The house was his alone, and he liked it that way. No one talking at him, no one watching him. He felt that people always disapproved when they saw him eat. A fat kid.

"Poor thing! It can't be glandular though, look at the way he shovels down that food!"

He could understand. It made him uncomfortable to watch fat people eat. Mouths too small, cheeks bulging, they seemed to hunch over their plates, shiny eyes riveted on the food. He made a point when he was eating with other people to sit up straight and appear disinterested.

But now he was alone and interested. He took an enormous bite from the sandwich. The peanut butter was very sticky and it cemented his jaws together. He opened his mouth wide in order to free his teeth. It didn't work. The wedge of sandwich was so large there was little room for maneuver.

The doorbell rang. Still struggling with the inert mass of peanut butter, bread, jam and banana, he got up, walked across the room and opened the door.

A small man carrying a large suitcase stood on the path looking up at Harold. He wore a suit and tie. Sweat trickled from under a black fedora and ran down the sides of his face. He seemed twitchy, confused and angry. Behind him in the street a cab was just pulling away.

He slammed down the suitcase and took a couple of short aggressive steps towards Harold, almost forcing the boy back into the house.

"What the hell's going on here?" he demanded. "And, who the hell are you?"

Harold was still trying to clear his mouth.

"What have I told you, Harold? Not once, a hundred times. Not with your mouth full! Are you listening?"

"Haron — ah, Abel-mum," was the best he could manage.

The man stared in disgust at Harold's half-open mouth.

"What?" he said sharply. "Damn it, I can't understand a word!"

In a panic Harold attempted to disengage himself from the sandwich's dental embrace. He swallowed. Nothing happened. He tried again. This time it worked, but the lump only made it halfway down. He began to choke. The man stepped back in alarm as Harold clutching his throat and making desperate chunting sounds staggered down the path towards him.

"UhAh, UhAh, UhAh ... WOO-LAH!!"

The man's leg caught against the suitcase and he stumbled backward. Just then Harold launched a sodden projectile of peanut butter, bread, jam and banana. It hit the man square in the chest, hung to his shirt for a moment before dropping to the ground. A few seconds later it was sizzling on the griddle-hot flagstones.

Harold leaned against the side of the house breathing hard, his face a rich scarlet. The man sat on the ground looking at the brown stain on his shirt and shaking his head slowly from side to side. His hat had fallen off. Harold noticed that he was almost totally bald.

"Enid! ENID! Please Enid! Come quick!"

It was his grandfather. He sounded in genuine distress. Harold rushed into the house, slamming the door closed behind him. The little bald-headed guy would just have to wait.

* * *

"I'm sorry, lady, but I can't pull you out. The flat's gone right down into the sand there. Look, you can see yourself. Could damage the axle if I tried to move it. We'll just have to wait for the tow truck. You wanna sit down in my car?"

"But I've got to get to the airport!"

"Relax, willya. Please."

"Can't you just run me over there? Look, it's only a couple a minutes. It's very important."

The big policeman shook his head.

"It's more than my job is worth, and anyway with that bump on your head you should be going to the hospital, not the airport."

"I keep telling you. I'm fine. I was out for a few seconds that's all. Don't make a federal case out of it. OK?"

"OK, lady," he said throwing up his hands. "OK. OK. I don't wanna argue with you."

She checked her watch. A quarter after twelve. Only forty-five minutes late. The plane might have been delayed, she thought hopefully. Or he might still be waiting. That was a less hopeful thought, for if there was one thing that Archie really hated it was waiting around. If they went to a restaurant and they couldn't get a table right away he was out the door.

"Life's too damn short for standing around like a mug. We got better things to do. Right, babe?"

She limped over and sat down in the police car.

"Do you mind?" she asked, hand on the rearview mirror.

"Be my guest, lady."

She adjusted the mirror so she could see her face.

"Oh, Lord! Oh Sweet God!"

"You alright?" asked the cop, bending to look in the window.

"Yeah. It's just how I look, that's not alright!"

Her hat had come off and her hair, which she had so painstakingly arranged, was a tangled mess. An ugly red welt had come up over her left eye, and there seemed to be swelling around both eyes. She reached up to touch the bruise but quickly pulled her hand away. It was painful. There were runs in her stockings and her new dress was torn across the shoulder, exposing the white strap of her bra.

Welcome to Palm Springs, Archie Blatt.

It was like a blast furnace in the open police car. She began to sob. Trails of black mascara ran down her cheeks.

"Please, lady, take it easy willya."

The policeman fidgeted nervously by the side of his car.

"Lady? You listening in there? I know I shouldn't be doing this, but it's being Sunday and lunch time and, well, old Jerry might not get that truck out here so quick, and it's so dang blasted hot and all, I guess I could take you up there to the airport, if..."

"Take me to the airport?" she cried. "The airport!? That's the last place in the world I want to go looking like this!"

Enid knew it was all hopeless. Utterly beyond recovery. She couldn't stop crying.

* * *

"Enid! God, please! Enid!"

"What's the matter?" asked Harold, hovering anxiously over the his grandfather, who was sitting on the side of the bed, swollen hands resting limply on his knees.

"Where's Enid?" Abe asked, his face screwed up in pain.

"Still not back."

"I can't get up," he said in tears, weakly hitting at his legs. "Can't. They don't work. I try to push. Try and nothing happens and I've gotta go to the bathroom! Please!"

He held out a shaky hand towards Harold. The boy reached down, put the old man's arm over his shoulder and lifted him up. Then slowly he helped him down the hall into the bathroom. Someone, most likely the bald guy, was banging on the front door. He ignored it.

Harold stood his grandfather against the sink and pulled down his pajama pants. The pale legs quivered unsteadily. He lowered him gently onto the toilet. The old man moaned with relief and let go a string of wet farts, followed immediately by the splattering rush of diarrhea. The stench billowed out of the toilet bowl and filled the room. Harold held his breath and pushed open the window. It did little to clear the air.

Blue Valley Y-Camp! Good-bye, good-bye, good-bye. The unremitting odor of fresh shit wafting up between the rough board seats. No privacy. Other kids yelling and shouting. He had to be alone on the toilet or he couldn't go. It had been very tough for him at Blue Valley Y-Camp.

Head sunk forward onto his chest, Abe began to cry softly.

"Please,"Harold begged, sitting on the side of the bath and putting out a tentative hand to pat Abe on the shoulder. "It's going to be alright. Don't cry, Granddad. Come on, don't."

God, thought Harold, I sound like Aunt Enid! That surprised him, as did his being able to cope with actually touching the old man's increasingly putrefactive body. Not that he liked doing it. He didn't. But it wasn't as bad as he had imagined.

Outside, the banging was getting more frenzied.

"It's not," said Abe distractedly. "Not going to be alright. I'm dying, Harold. How can that be alright? Can't walk, got no strength at all, have to be washed like a little baby, nobody knows what this kind of dying is like."

"I gotta get the door now," said Harold, standing up. "Be back in a second."

Abe grabbed for him. Fingers rasped feebly against Harold's forearm.

"Don't leave me, son! Please don't leave me here by myself!"

"But there's someone knocking."

He let go of Harold. His arms flopped to his sides.

"Just like that daughter of mine," he said petulantly, "leaving me by myself in the house. A sick man. No feelings for what I'm going through, no feelings at all."

"It's not like that," Harold said. "She had to go out to pick up her friend. That's all. She'll be back soon."

"You say," retorted Abe. "Covering up for her. That's it. She doesn't care about her father. No one cares. An old man, that's all. A dying old man. In the way. You don't think I know that? Huh? You hear what I'm saying? I know that. Of course I know that."

It's unfair, thought Harold. Aunt Enid is killing herself for this guy. Feeding him, washing him, cleaning up his shit, and all he can do is bitch and moan about her.

The banging stopped.

He looked at his watch. It was 12:30. Aunt Enid was very late. He supposed that the plane could have been delayed. It was only then that he realized who the man at the front door was.

Ignoring Abe's protestations he ran out of the bathroom. He reached the front door and flung it open. There was no one there.

Harold walked out of the house and into the road. He looked in both directions. Empty.

The midday desert sun reflected harshly off the white sand. He stood there for a minute then went back inside and closed the door.

* * *

"You mind telling me just exactly what the FUCK is going on here?"

Rumpled, sweaty, furious and hatless, Archie Blatt was waiting for Harold in the living room. The patio door was open behind him.

"Ha - Ha - Harold Abelstein."

Archie glared up at the boy, uncomprehending.

"What's that?" he snapped. "Huh? What's that?"

"My name?" answered Harold unsurely.

"Harold! Please, Harold!" his grandfather cried out from the bathroom.

"Excuse me just one second," said Harold backing away towards the hall.

"And, who the hell is that?" roared Archie, in despair.

Without answering, Harold lumbered off. Archie followed.

"Harold!"

"It's OK. I'm here, I'm here. Take it easy."

Abe was still sitting on the toilet, a concertina of pajamas around his ankles.

"Where did you go? Leaving me like this. Please, Harold, I want to lie down now."

"Sure. Come on. Have you um, you know?"

"Wiped?" Abe asked, innocently.

"Uh-huh."

"Yeah," he cackled, "I've wiped! God damn, have I wiped! Used almost half the roll as well!"

Having a crap had obviously revived his grandfather's spirits.

Harold pulled up Abe's pants, tightened the draw string around his waist.

"Give me your arm," he said.

"Hello there," said Abe, as they squeezed passed Archie in the narrow hallway.

The small man stood dumbstruck. After a minute he cautiously put his head around the doorway to Enid's dressing room.

"Come in, come in," Abe said, waving Archie in from the hallway.

Harold was by the bed, smiling lamely and shifting his weight from one foot to the other.

So this was the guy Aunt Enid wanted him to be good friends with? Wonderful! Fat chance now, he thought. First I puke on him, then slam the door in his face. A great start! Where the hell is Aunt Enid?

Archie walked wearily into the room as if he might at any moment step into quicksand or fall down an open manhole. He looked around him at the walls. The roses seemed to reassure him that he was in the right place. Then he focused on Harold.

"Harold?" he asked.

Harold nodded. Archie relaxed slightly. His mouth crinkled into a knowing smile.

"Sure," he said, "Harold. Harold Abelstein. Sure. You're Enid's nephew, aren't you? Her sister's son from up in Los Angeles. I got it now. How you doing?"

They shook hands.

"Fine," said Harold, pleased that at least Archie knew who he was.

"Listen, Harold," Archie said, taking him by the elbow and glancing uneasily at the bed, "can I have a word with you in private?"

"Hi," called Abe from behind Harold. "Abe Cohen's the name."

"Hi there," Archie called back over his shoulder as he propelled Harold towards the door. "Nice to see you. Excuse us for a minute, will you?"

"I don't mind," said Abe, sounding as if he did.

* * *

"Enid's father?"

"Yeah, that's right."

Archie sat down on the couch. He took a handkerchief from his pocket and mopped the sweat off his head and face. He leaned forward, hands on his knees.

"Her father, huh? What's he doing here?"

"Well," said Harold, "I don't know really. He's sort of sick."

Archie paused, picked a white thread off his pants.

"He staying here? You mean, permanently staying? Here?"

Harold didn't think it was really any of Archie's business. He figured if Enid wanted to, she would tell him. After all, he was her friend.

"Sort of," he answered.

"Sort of," Archie repeated under his breath.

He took off his jacket and loosened his tie.

"Yeah. OK. Let's move on a little. I thought she told me once that her father disappeared or something like that when she was a kid. You mean he turned up here? Out of the blue?"

Harold shrugged. Archie seemed to be having a hard time getting a grip on things. Harold knew he wasn't being very helpful. He didn't care.

"It smells awful in there," Archie ventured.

"I suppose so," replied Harold.

Archie looked at Harold questioningly. Nothing. He tried another tack.

"And you? What? Here for a visit? Summer vacation? You know, I usually don't come out this time of year. Probably why I've never seen you before."

"Yeah."

Archie raised his eyes up to the ceiling as if looking for divine intervention.

"Uh-huh. I see. Good," he said, leaning back and crossing his short legs. "So, where's your aunt then?"

"She went to pick you up at the airport. About an hour ago."

"Well, as you can see," he said, spreading his arms, "she didn't."

"Yeah."

"Right. Probably just missed me. Be here any minute, I expect. Actually, she should have been here before now."

Archie frowned.

"Shopping maybe? Yeah, probably had to do some shopping on the way back. Listen, Harold, I've just got to clean up."

He pointed to the brown stain on his shirt. Harold blushed.

"I've also got to call the office in St. Louis. Damn business. No escape from it. Don't go away."

He got up. As he passed in front of Enid's dressing room, Abe called out to him. Archie waved, said something Harold couldn't hear and continued on into Aunt Enid's bedroom. He closed the door behind him.

* * *

"We was just passing by and thought we'd look in. You know, to say howdy."

In her blood-red toreador pants and white puffed-sleeved blouse Harold thought Charlene looked like an enormous lamb chop. He couldn't shake the image. It was worrying.

"How you doing, Champ? Still knocking 'em dead?"

Big John slapped Harold on the arm. The lamb chop's husband was also worrying, as well as a pain in the butt.

Not for the first time since he had come to the desert, Harold urgently wished he was somewhere far, far away. Los Angeles would have been nice. It was Sunday. If he was in LA, and if he had the money, he could go to Fairfax and get some fresh bagels, maybe Cantor's for lox and eggs. Then in the afternoon up to Hollywood Boulevard for a matinee. The deep velvet seats at Grauman's Chinese. Afterwards across to Brown's and a hot fudge sundae with chocolate ice cream. City dreams.

They were shattered by the twang of Charlene's voice.

"Tell me, Harold," she said, pushing up close to him, "Archie arrived yet?"

"Yeah," Harold replied, stepping back and pointing towards the bedroom. "He's on the phone."

"Actually," Charlene said, in what was for her a whisper, "we come by to sorta help Enid out. You know?"

Harold couldn't imagine how, or for that matter why.

"It's just sometimes," she continued, "when you gotta do these kinda things, it's better if there's other folk around to soak up some of the heat from the fire, if you catch my meaning."

She winked at him. He didn't know why she was winking, what she was talking about. Exactly what did Enid have to do? More important, where was she? She'd been gone for more than an hour and a half. He was starting to worry. What if she never came back?

He closed his eyes and heard his mother's scream, glass breaking, felt the sickening jolts as the car bounced and rolled over, again and again. Pasadena. Too much smog in Pasadena.

"Harold! Harold!"

He fled from the living room.

"What's going on out there?" Abe demanded. "You said you'd come straight back."

Harold told him about Charlene and John. Abe didn't seem very interested.

"I saw Enid's friend walk right into her bedroom," Abe said indignantly. "You hear what I'm saying? Right in he walked and closed the door, liked he owned the place. That's no friend, Harold. No. More like a *boyfriend*. You hear what I'm saying? Boyfriend!"

Harold knew that already. Aunt Enid had told him.

"And, how old do you think he is? Huh? Must be sixty if he's a day. Maybe more. You know something, that's not right. It isn't. Too old for her. Old enough to be her damn father. Look at me. Sixty-five years old. And, I *am* her father."

Harold knew that as well.

Abe shook his head sadly.

"My little girl. Little Enid." Then more anxiously, "Where is she? Where's Enid?"

"On her way back, I suppose," said Harold, evasively.

The old man sat up in the bed. He studied Harold closely. Finally he shouted at him with unexpected vehemence, saliva spraying from his mouth.

"Bull-shit! Bull-shit! Bull-shit! She's gone, isn't she? Run away. I can see it there, there in your sorry fat face! Couldn't take it any longer, could she? Skipped town, I bet. Leaving me on my own. Having her revenge. You hear what I'm saying? Revenge. You know why? Do you? Because of the damn Depression. That's all it was. The damn Depression! What could I do? I ask you? What? It wasn't my fault, damn it! I wasn't my fault. It wasn't."

He fell back on his pillow exhausted.

"Fat face," thought Harold. He supposed he knew that too.

"Do you need anything," he asked.

Abe didn't answer. He turned his head towards the wall and the roses.

Back in the living room, Charlene and John had settled down on the couch.

"Where's Enid at?" asked Charlene.

"That's exactly what I'd like to know," said Archie, who at that moment strode into the living room behind Harold.

"Why hello, Charlene, John. Nice to see you both."

Harold moved to one side. The men shook hands. Charlene pecked Archie on the cheek. All old friends thought Harold, relieved that he wouldn't be expected to do anything. His relief was short-lived.

"So wadda you think of our Harold then?" asked Charlene, looking at Archie and then giving Harold a flirtatious flutter of false eyelashes.

"Isn't he just a lamb chop?"

Harold gagged.

Archie was sizing him up as if seriously considering Charlene's proposition, but before he could answer the front was flung open and Enid limped in followed closely by a very large policeman.

It Makes Me Think I'm On My Last Go 'Round

Enid's entry was met with a stony hush as everyone in the room took in the bruises, the disheveled hair, the torn clothes. She, too, froze in front of the unexpected and unwanted audience. She looked from one to the other. Faces seemed to her to be suspended, floating above their bodies, enlarged and grainy like badly developed photographs. Charlene, John, Harold, Archie. She wanted to get away from them, to run into her room and hide. They didn't give her the chance. Everyone started to talk at once.

"Oh honey! What...? How did...? Are you...?"

Charlene was the first to go over to her. She put a protective arm around Enid's shoulder.

"Honey! Oh honey!" she kept repeating.

"It's OK," pleaded Enid, trying to wriggle out from under the weight of Charlene's embrace, "I'll be OK. It looks worse then it is. Had a flat tire. That's all. Went off the road and got a little bump on the head."

She saw Archie watching her from across the room. He seemed rooted to the carpet. Realizing how battered and unglamorous she must look she caught his eye, shrugged hopefully and gave him a self-deprecating smile. It was a moment or two before he returned it and then it came back at only half power, the eye contact unsure. It was as if he needed more time to think about what he was seeing.

What little remained of Enid's spirits crumbled away. If he couldn't get by this, she said to herself, how was he going to handle the rest? No way was the simple answer to that. No way at all. She took a deep shuddering breath.

"If you're OK," said the policeman, "I'll be getting on."

"Oh, yeah," said Enid, trying to force the deadness out of her voice. "And, thanks very much."

"Sure thing," he said.

Then he spied Harold across the room. He grinned broadly, using all his teeth.

"Well, if it ain't my old friend Harold Abel-*Stein*. You keeping outta trouble like I told you to, boy?"

Enid looked questioning from the policeman to Harold and back. How did he know Harold, she wondered? More trouble? Those thoughts were swiftly pushed aside by the blinding anger which boiled up at the over-deliberate way the policeman had pronounced Harold's last name. It was that anti-Semitic edge she had heard so often in Palm Springs. It was that edge and all that went with it which had made her trade in Cohen for Carlson. Nothing up front, no kike, hebe or shenny, but a crystal clear message just the same. The Shadow Mountain Club, Smoke Tree Ranch, Thunderbird Country Club, The Tennis Club. The bastards! She had to choke back the frustration. There was really nothing she could say. How could she complain about an edge?

"Yes, sir," replied Harold, embarrassed and blushing.

"That's a good boy," he said heartily, then turning to the others, "If you folks'll excuse me."

He touched the peak of his cap and walked out.

Big Jim and Big John. Now all we need to make a complete set, thought Harold despairingly, is Big Earl. He felt a lot better when the front door closed.

He was also pleased that his aunt had come back, although it frightened him that she was so badly beaten up. Out of control almost. Unrecognizable. Then there was what Charlene had said. Some mysterious thing that Aunt Enid had to do and that Charlene was there to help her with.

"Come and sit down, honey," Charlene said, hovering next to her friend.

Enid wanted to be by herself, but she let Charlene lead her over to the couch. She sat down stiffly. Her eyes were throbbing, her ankle hurt, and she was getting a headache. She also felt the familiar dull pulling ache low down in her belly.

She'd been feeling premenstrual for a couple of days, but it hadn't seemed as bad as usual. No tiredness or depression, not even any of the backache she often got. Maybe she had been too preoccupied to notice. She was still preoccupied but could no longer ignore the fact that her period was about to start.

What a time to get the curse, she thought bitterly. Archie is going to he thrilled! ... To hell with him! Selfish bastard! ... It's not really his fault ... Oh shit!

Despite everything she felt she had to go through at least some of the motions. It was expected. Archie expected it.

"I'm really sorry, Archie," Enid said with a tired sigh, "I was on my way and..."

He held up his hands.

"Hey, babe!" he said, coming over to her, "Please! It's no problem at all. It's you we got to worry about. Gee, you sure you're OK?"

He gave her a hesitant kiss on the check, his lips coming away blackened by mascara.

She began to weep. Archie put his arm around her. His attention only made her more miserable.

"Well," said John, nervously smoothing his moustache with one finger, "if everything is under control, maybe we should hit the road? What do you say, Charlene?"

"Oh, shut up, will you?" his wife shot back. "Can't you see everything ain't under no damn control?"

"Please ... Charlene," Enid managed between sobs, "It's OK... I'll be alright. You go with John... I'll call... later."

Charlene seemed unsure.

"But, honey, your poor face..."

"You heard the little lady, Charlene. Come on now, let's just vamoose."

Big John took hold of his wife's arm and tried gently to pull her towards the door. Charlene didn't budge.

Harold saw a stick insect hanging onto the side of a gigantic lamb chop and immediately let loose a snorting, high-pitched giggle.

He put his hand to his mouth as soon he realized who it was he heard laughing. It became airlessly quiet. Everyone was staring at him, slack-jawed with disbelief, as if he had done something heinously sacrilegious. He stared back, similarly slack-jawed.

"Harold! Harold!"

Harold ducked his head and stumbled out of the room. He suddenly had an overwhelming desire to see his grandfather.

* * *

"Let me at least call the doctor and have him come by and see you, babe? I don't like the look of that lump."

"No, Archie. Please. I'll be fine and I can tell there's nothing broken. What's the point?"

"Maybe a concussion or something like that? Anyway, there's no harm in the doctor having a look, is there?"

"You obviously haven't seen the doctor," she said.

She took his handkerchief and dabbed at her face and looked down at the residue of lipstick and mascara staining the white cloth.

John and Charlene had gone, and Harold was in with Abe. They were alone together. He moved closer to her on the couch until their legs were touching and put his hand on her thigh.

"Gee, babe, I missed you," he whispered in the special, childlike voice he reserved for their lovemaking.

Tired, sore and premenstrual, Enid was definitely not in the mood.

"Please, Archie," she said testily, pulling away, "let me clean up and change, OK? Then we've got to talk about.things."

He pulled his hand away as if he had had an electric shock, stood up and glanced uneasily towards the hall. There was no one there.

"Oh, sure, babe. Yeah. You go ahead. Sorry."

Abe shouted as she passed his room.

"Enid! Will you come here a minute? I got..."

"Not now, please!"

She went into her room and pushed the door closed.

It was worse than in the car mirror. The bump was now the size of a golf ball and the swelling around her eyes had gone a livid purple black. Mascara streaks, her mouth an untidy puddle of lipstick, hair clotted and tangled. Terrified, she backed away from her reflection, afraid it might step out of the mirror and follow her. Her legs hit the edge of the bed and she sat down heavily. A monster, she thought. An ugly, ugly monster!

It was about five minutes before she calmed down enough to look at herself again. Not a monster this time, more like a battered clown. Still it wasn't good.

Well, she told herself, maybe it's not all that terrible. After all, Archie had seemed affectionate enough — too affectionate — after he got over the initial shock. Why? ... Horny? That was alright, she could understand horny, but what she didn't understand was why he would want her looking like she did. It was disgusting. *She* wouldn't want her.

In the bathroom she bathed her face, washing off all the damaged make-up. The cool water made the bruises hurt but it was refreshing. Sitting on the toilet, eyes closed, she brushed out her hair, counting the strokes on each side as her mother had done. Although it pulled at her sore face, the slow repetitive action relaxed her. When she finished, she tied up her hair and applied fresh lipstick. A very large pair of sunglasses covered the bruised eyes. She took off her torn dress and put on slacks and a blouse. The monster had been temporarily vanquished.

Now the only thing left to do was to explain everything to Archie. He had met Harold, had seen her father, but how much did he know about what was going on? Had he pumped Harold for information? If he had, she couldn't imagine he had much success. To get the time of day out of Harold was virtually impossible.

It was not working out as she had planned. She hadn't even had the five minutes from the airport.

Archie Blatt.

Had he had his usual erection when he got off the plane? All the way from Los Angeles, thinking about making love to his woman, Archie Blatt's woman. And what happens? The woman doesn't turn up. Waiting, having to take a cab, his erection drooping in the desert heat. Maybe starting to rise again as the cab turns off the main road, stiffening in anticipation, getting harder as they pull up to the house. Then bang! Major collapse. The house is full of strangers, one of them dying, the other an over-sized kid who doesn't say two words and giggles out of context. Charlene and John. A leering anti-Semitic cop who resembles King Kong. And her, Archie Blatt's fancy woman, looking as if she'd just gone ten rounds with a clothes dryer. Sexy. Very sexy. Just what he paid for.

Gift wrapped. She smiled. It was so terrible it had to be funny.

A clutching stomach cramp unexpectedly hit. It wasn't at all funny.

"Not now!" she cried out loud, doubling over.

She went back into the bathroom, inserted a Tampax and took three aspirins. Then she lay down on the bed, pulled her knees to her chest and waited for the pain to recede. Muffled voices, Abe's mostly, came from across the hall mixed with the low unsyncopated clatter of the water cooler. At least, she thought thankfully, there's no loud music. Just a dying old man blabbering. She tried to weigh it up, but couldn't. Another cramp interrupted her thoughts.

"Damn! Damn!"

It wasn't fair. Why did she have to go through this crap every month? She knew why. It was still unfair.

And outside her room?

Abe and Archie and Harold. All waiting for her. She felt grindingly tired. She closed her eyes.

* * *

The telephone call was from St. Louis. It woke her up. She called Archie into the bedroom, and he yelled down the phone for ten minutes. Each word vibrated in Enid's head like a steel ball dropped into an empty metal bucket.

"Can you believe that?" he said, slamming down the receiver.

He gave Enid a questioning stare. She tried to look sympathetic. It wasn't easy. She felt awful.

"You leave them alone for a couple of days and the whole operation goes haywire. Fabric doesn't come in, suddenly cutters I've had for twenty-five years, they can't cut patterns. The workrooms don't deliver. The button man sends all the wrong sizes. 'So, cut the holes a little bigger,' he says. A real joker, huh? And, the designer? The designer won't talk to me. He's too upset. He's upset! Jesus! You know, babe, if I had it all to do over it wouldn't be in the rag trade. You can bet your ass on that. Not the rag trade. You gotta be completely *meshugge* to be in this business."

He got up from the bed and started to pace.

"You know what it would be?"

Enid knew. She nodded. It didn't spare her the explanation.

"Banking. That's it, banking. You know why?"

She knew why. What's more, Archie knew she knew why. That wasn't the point.

"Because the bastards own everything. Who do you think I work for? Right. The bank. That's who I work for. Paying off the goddamned overdraft! Begging them for one more month. And what do they do? Do they have to worry if the Spring collection sells? Do they my ass! Can you see them staying up nights thinking what they'll do if the union makes trouble? Hell no they don't! Nine to five. That's what they got. Nine to five. Push some papers, make some calls, hassle a few poor schmucks like me and then home to the wife and kids. Easy. Yeah, babe, banking is definitely what I should have done."

He sat on the bed and then immediately was on his feet again.

"Then there's all the other people I work for, I stay up nights for. You know. Yeah. What would they do if I didn't find their damn salaries on the tenth of every damn month? Right out of a job they'd be. In the street. But, do they appreciate that? Do they take care of things when I'm away? ... Then to top it off..."

Enid tuned him out. Was he always like this she wondered? It hadn't occurred to her before how much Archie complained about his business. To her surprise, she found herself getting angry with him. Here I am, she thought, bruised and battered *and* bleeding and that's all he can talk about.

" '...Mr. Blatt? Melvin,' I said, 'Melvin you don't'... Aah, what the hell. Who cares? Why should *I* care anymore? You know something, babe? I got something to tell you... I..."

His voice trailed off and as if a fog had lifted he seemed to see Enid for the first time. He smiled sheepishly.

"Oh, hey, babe, I'm sorry. Going on like that and you lying there all banged up, feeling lousy."

He went over, sat next to her on the bed and took her hand.

"How do you feel, babe? Any better?"

"I got my period."

"Oh," he replied nonplussed. "That's uh... tough at a time like this, if you know what I mean."

He let go of her hand. She gave a short harsh laugh. Archie

fidgeted uneasily with the end of his tie.

"So," he said, "I see your father's turned up out of the blue, huh?"

She wasn't ready. Here it was on the line and she was not even close to ready.

"Will you shut the blinds, Archie. The light's hurting my eyes."

* * *

The thin wire dug into his hands as he lifted the bale. He balanced it on his knees just like Earl had shown him, bent his legs and threw the hay forward onto the top of the stack.

"Don't fight it, son," Big Earl had said. "Let the weight work for you."

It hadn't taken him long to learn the technique. Once the rhythm came, it felt good swinging the bales up.

"You sure are one strong dude," Little Earl had commented as they worked side by side building the stack outside the tin-roofed barn. "Now we just gotta get you fixed up with a half-way decent hat."

They both laughed.

They were almost finished and Harold felt great. Tired, sweaty, and itchy from the dust and the hay, but unexpectedly great. Like the horseback riding and helping clean out the stalls, such physical satisfaction was a completely new experience. If he hadn't been forced to do it he would never have believed he could enjoy it. This time he hadn't even minded the static rumble of the country music coming from the radio in Earl's truck. It seemed to fit.

Once again, his visit to the stables had been prompted by the need to get away. This time from his grandfather and the added tension which Archie seemed to have brought with him. Harold didn't understand exactly what it was all about, but Aunt Enid was uncharacteristically edgy and bad tempered.

His grandfather had fallen asleep in the middle of some rambling incoherent account of an unemployed butcher, the thirty-eighth person, he said, to have admitted dismembering the Black Dahlia in LA in 1947. He was on the point of giving Harold the full details of the other thirty-seven when he dozed off.

The door to Aunt Enid's room was closed. Harold stood in the hallway listening. He could hear them talking in low voices. He knocked softly. It went quiet inside. There was no answer. He waited and then knocked a little harder. After a minute or so Archie opened the door, but only a couple of inches. He looked extremely annoyed.

"What's the problem, Harold?" he asked in a whisper.

"Uh, can I talk to my Aunt Enid?"

"She's resting right now. Can I do something for you?"

"No. That's alright, forget it."

Harold turned away. He didn't see why he should have to go through Archie to get to his aunt. The guy had been there only a couple of hours and already he was blocking the door. He knew then that he could never be "good friends" with him. Anyway, Harold told himself, he's too old to have as a real friend.

"Harold?"

It was Aunt Enid. Reluctantly, Archie opened the door fully. She was lying on the bed. The room was dark.

"What is it now, Harold?" she asked in an exasperated voice.

"I wanna go out for a while," he said, staring doggedly at his shoes. "The stables."

There was a pause.

"In case you didn't notice, Harold, I'm feeling like death here. Can't you see that? And, who's going to take care of... Oh, I don't care! Go! Go! Go out if you want to. Just leave me alone now. Please!"

More and more like his mother. The voice, the mode of attack, the guilt, the whole routine. He had wanted to tell her that whatever it was, it wasn't his fault, that he hadn't done anything. Experience told him the only thing to do was go. He went.

He thought he might be able to ride, but Earl and his father were stacking hay. He couldn't refuse to help.

"You stack a mean bale, cowboy," said Big Earl, smacking him roughly on the back. "Come on, let me buy you two boys a drink."

They sat on the steps of the tack room in the shade and sipped their Cokes. No one said a word. Harold felt comfortable with that. He couldn't say the same about what was coming from the Philco.

It Makes Me Think I'm On My Last Go 'Round

Now the ceremony has started
And I'll wed your bother, Don.
Would you wish us happiness forever
... Dear John.

* * *

Harold had knocked as she was explaining to Archie about him and her father. She felt terrible for yelling at him. Mouth dropped open, eyes widened, poor Harold had been dumbstruck by her outburst. Pushed further away, deeper into his teenage shell. She could see that Archie, too, was taken aback. A harridan with the curse. An awful, totally irredeemable woman.

Why am I doing this to myself? she asked, resenting her own thoughts. What have I done to either of them? Really done? Nothing. A bad mother? A bad wife? Or for that matter, a bad daughter? Impossible. I'm not Harold's mother, not Archie's wife and not really Abe Cohen's daughter. That's just how they treat me. And even if I was? Where's *my* return from it all? Only on empties, maybe. Sure, she thought, you only get a real return on empties. Her womb was still sore with cramp, and her head ached.

Not looking up, shoulders slumped against the world, Harold left the room. He didn't close the door.

"Well," said Archie, with an uneasy laugh, "that's that, I suppose."

"I suppose," Enid echoed bleakly.

They fell silent. The back door slammed shut. Harold had gone out.

"Alright," said Archie thoughtfully.

"So, what else could I do? I am his only relative."

He hesitated.

"Nothing, babe, you did right, I guess."

It sounded hollow to Enid, as if he had resigned himself to making the buttonholes bigger. She couldn't be sure. But, for the moment she didn't care. She was relieved to have finally told him about Harold and her father. Now it was his move.

* * *

"I hope you don't mind me saying so, but don't you think you're too old for my daughter? At least, that's my personal opinion, you know, for what it's worth, that is. What are you, late fifties maybe? Sixty? Huh? Whatever. Still, that's more than twenty years older. Twenty years! What's the matter, you couldn't find someone your own age?"

He looked Archie up and down.

"And, you're too short for her. She's a big woman, my Enid. A tall woman. What are you five-five? Five-six? She's five-eight, maybe taller. Too short, too old. Doesn't fit."

Archie stood at the foot of the bed with his mouth open. He moved his lips a few times but nothing came out.

"What's the matter with you?" asked Abe sharply, then in a more distracted tone, "I don't even know who you are."

"Listen," said Archie finally finding his voice. "I'm not here for a damn lecture. I'm here to see if you need anything. And, I'm *only* here because Enid asked me."

"So what's wrong with her? She can't look after her own father? Or the boy, that Harold. What do I need with strangers?"

"Harold's out, Enid doesn't feel well, so what you've got is me. Me. Short and old, but that's all there is right now. OK?"

"What's the matter with her?" asked Abe suspiciously.

"Nothing. She's tired."

"Tired? That must be some kind of tired if she has to send a stranger?"

"Listen, Mr. Cohen," said Archie impatiently "Do you need anything or don't you?"

"Maybe I do," he said haughtily, "then again, maybe I don't."

Archie threw up his hands.

"What is it? You want me to guess?"

"I don't like your tone," complained Abe, sounding hurt.

"My tone? My goddamn tone!? I come in here to ask if you need anything and what do I get? 'You're too old, you're too short' and 'I don't like strangers.' And now it's my tone you don't like. Give me a break will you?"

"From St. Louis?" Abe asked innocently.

"What do you mean? ...Yeah, St. Louis. So?"

"Ever see Musial play?"

"Baseball? I got a business to run. I don't have time for baseball."

Abe ignored his answer.

"I saw him play once. In Chicago, Wrigley Field. Yeah, he was really something that day. Two homers. Two. Yeah, Stan the Man... Stan the Man."

"Mr. Cohen?"

"What?"

"For the last time, do you need anything?"

"I want to see Enid," Abe said petulantly.

Archie's voice filled with tight impatience. He spoke very slowly, very deliberately.

"I told you, she's tired right now. Tell me and I'll get whatever it is."

"Enid. I want to see Enid."

Abe folded his arms, and as best he could he turned his back on Archie.

"Mr. Cohen! Be reasonable... Jesus H. Christ! I do not believe this is happening!"

Abe began to sob.

"I want Enid. I want Enid... Is that too much for a dying man to ask? I want my daughter. Enid! Enid!"

Archie started to say something but didn't. Defeated, he left the room without a backward glance at the old man.

* * *

"OK, OK. You can stop it now, I'm here. What is it?"

He beckoned to her with a feeble wave. She approached the bed. The smell of urine had become much worse. Like a fine mist, it enveloped her father. It seemed to Enid as if his body was becoming more insubstantial by the hour, evaporating into a cloud of urine.

"Please, Enid," he said in a whisper, looking over her shoulder at Archie, who was watching from the doorway, "I've gotta go to the bathroom."

Enid stared at her father, struggling with her annoyance and pity.

"So, what's wrong with Archie?"

"I told him already," replied Abe indignantly, "he's too old, too short."

"You told him WHAT?" she asked incredulously.

"Too old for you," he repeated, "too short for you."

Enid looked at Archie. He nodded and gave a wry smile.

"What!?... How!?..." she stammered.

"Can I go to the bathroom now?"

"It's none of your damn business!" she shouted at him.

Abe seemed puzzled. He licked his lips.

"What do you mean none of my business? Please, Enid. I really must..."

"I'd like to know where the hell do you come off with saying stuff like that?"

Abe was staring intently at her.

"Your face," he said in a frightened voice. "What happened to your face?"

"I asked you... What are...? Nothing, I had a slight accident."

"You should be more careful," he said, shaking his head dolefully, "Young people, they never see the dangers. Reckless. In a hurry. All the time in a hurry. What would happen to me? You've got obligations here, Enid. Obligations."

Enid sighed deeply. The only thing she wanted to do was lie down and have some peace and quiet. To concentrate on her own pain and discomfort and not have to worry about anyone else's. No Harold, no Archie and especially no Abe Cohen. Only herself, only Enid.

"I didn't want strangers," Abe whined. "Why do I have to have strangers?"

He is my father. He is dying.

She helped him up. Although he weighed almost nothing, because of her own weakened condition Enid tottered slightly as he leaned against her. His fingers gripped tightly onto her arm. She could see his scalp through the damp strands of hair, feel the fluttering beat of his heart. She was suddenly overtaken by a dull, heavy sadness. It washed over her, blotting out the anger and the self-pity.

"Do you need me, babe?" Archie asked unsurely.

"That's a very interesting question," she replied, forcing a laugh to hold off the tears.

* * *

Caught in the late afternoon shade, Enid and Archie were lying in the pool side by side on half-submerged air mattresses. Water covered stomach and chest, arms and legs, only their heads and feet were exposed to the hot desert air. Aspirins had muffled the pains from the bruises and from her period and, as it always did, the cool water was soothing her.

"Sure," said Archie, "I know what you mean, babe. He's a sick old man. They can talk crazy when they're like that. Don't worry about it, I understand."

Enid wondered if he did. She looked at him floating next to her. His air mattress was purple, and purple was obviously not Archie's color. If she was honest, she also had to admit that her father was probably right. Archie was too old and too short, as well as too married, something which, thankfully, her father didn't know about. Now she and Archie would have to pretend that he wasn't too old or too short, that what had been said was nothing but the ravings of a dying man.

"I know this wasn't at all what you were expecting, Archie. I'm sorry. But, like I said, it's only a temporary arrangement."

He pushed his hands through the water, the mattress swinging at right angles to Enid's.

"Yeah, I see that, babe. But, um... ah, about the kid, about Harold. After, well you know... after with your father, then he's going to come back here, right?"

"Yes."

She had explained it all to him before, but he was still probing, hoping somehow he would get a different answer. For Archie there was always the possibility of cutting the cloth another way so as to squeeze out one more garment.

"But even there, I mean," said Enid, not liking the pleading in her voice, "he is almost sixteen and he's got only two more years of high school. That's not much time, is it? Before we know it he'll be gone."

Was she apologizing or begging? Both, she decided and hated herself for it. Since Harold had arrived a few weeks before, the layers of protective skin which she had allowed to grow over her life had been peeled away one by one. With Archie's arrival she was down to the raw flesh. She didn't like what she felt or what she saw. If only, she thought, Norman hadn't missed that stupid freeway turnoff none of this would be happening.

"Sure," Archie replied without much conviction. "You're absolutely right, babe, that's no time all."

They floated in silence for a while. She wished she could see his eyes. Enid could sense that Archie was working out his next move, trying to get his phrasing just right. After what had happened with Harold and her father she expected the worst. What would come after that was still unclear in her mind. Once in a while, if she let it move in close, she caught glimpses of herself in a waitress's uniform, or with a green Safeway coat standing next to a cash register. A trailer, maybe out at that dump, the Sunshine Trailer Park, on the far side of Cathedral City. Harold filling up one narrow end of it with himself and his boxes of records. Her feet swollen from standing up all day, her skin going white. Getting fat and irritable in the heat. Lots of drinking in the local bar at night. No prospects. Old at forty. She tried for another set of images, but nothing came.

She cupped her hand in the pool and splashed the water onto her face.

* * *

If they call you a big man
'Cause you gotta lotta bottom land
If you kin to the President
And you help run the government
But if you're getting no attention
You're better off on a pension
If you ain't loving, then you ain't living.

"Oh yeah," said Harold, "she's alright... Well, I mean, I suppose she's not completely alright. That is, you see, she had sort of an accident this morning. Driving out to the airport."

Big Earl stopped drawing in the sand with a stick and looked a question over at Harold.

The boy shrugged.

"Just a bump on the head I think, black eye, you know, that sort of thing."

"That's too bad," said Big Earl, throwing the stick aside. "Damned good-looking woman, your aunt. Strung a little high though, don't you reckon?"

"I guess," Harold replied unsurely.

Faron Young faded out, and the radio announcer began talking about how everyone better get down to Blackstone Dodge before the end of the month if they didn't want to miss some once in a lifetime automotive bargains.

"She ain't married, is she?"

"No."

"Divorced?"

"No."

He picked up the stick again and began meticulously to scrape manure off the heels of his boots.

"How is it a woman that pretty never got herself hitched? That sure is one hell of a waste."

Both Earls laughed. Harold squirmed.

He didn't like it when men talked about his aunt. There was always a sexual edge that made him uneasy. And they seemed to want something from him as well. He didn't know what that was.

He hoped she would settle down and it would be like before; once Archie left, once his grandfather died. Surely the old man couldn't last much longer. The doctor had said a week at the most. Harold thought maybe he should feel guilty about wishing he was dead, but he didn't. Anyway, he didn't really wish he was dead, he just looked forward to getting away from John and Charlene and back into his own room. Aunt Enid had promised to paint over the roses.

It was not as if Abe Cohen was anyone he actually knew. He wasn't even a very nice person. In fact, thinking about it, Harold decided that he didn't like him very much at all. The way he got at Aunt Enid bothered him. She had to spend a lot of her time looking after her father. The old man sucked it up. A real vampire. At least now he spent most of the time asleep rather than talking incessantly as he had at first. Aunt Enid said he was fading away. Harold hoped she was right. He liked the idea of his grandfather "fading away". It sounded better than "dying".

Big Earl stood up and brushed off his Levis.

"Well," he said, "Can't sit around here all day jawing. Gotta be gettin' on. Now don't you forget to say howdy to your aunt for me, Harold."

"You bet," Harold replied.

He tapped his son on the arm.

"You going to clean up them saddles, boy?"

"I'm thinking on it, yes, sir."

"Glad to hear it," Big Earl laughed. "You think on it real good now. And when you're through thinking on it, then get your lame ass in there and put something down."

Little Earl grinned at his father and threw a punch which the older man easily ducked. He waved at the boys, got in his pickup and drove away.

Harold watched the exchange with envy. He and his father had never shared any kind of rough physical intimacy. The Abelsteins were neither a rough nor a particularly intimate family. Never before had Harold thought he might have wanted it to be. But, watching Earl and his father he suddenly missed his own father and all the things they hadn't been together and hadn't done together. He figured that was just about most things there were to be or to do.

Earl got up and put his hand on Harold's shoulder. He squeezed hard.

"Come on, Harold, ol' son, teach you how to clean up a saddle. Never know when it might come in handy for you to know something like that."

The boys went into the tack room. Earl stopped in front of the radio and held up his hand for Harold to be quiet.

"Stop right there. Now this here is a real good one, Harold," said Earl turning up the volume. "You listen up. Get yourself some music edu-cating."

Harold listened. It was Hank Thompson, who apparently didn't know God made honky-tonk angels.

It wasn't bad, Harold thought, at least not for a hick country song. A hell of a lot better than "Sixteen Tons" or "Dear John." He wondered if Earl knew what year it had come out and what color the label was.

* * *

"Gee," said Archie crinkling up his nose, "the kid smells awful bad. What's he been doing?"

Harold had just left the living room.

"Oh, that. The stables. Remember?"

Enid knew what he was thinking. "Horse shit in the living room, piss in the hall." It was all sliding away from her, gathering momentum and there was nothing she could do.

Harold had returned about ten minutes before. He asked if he could go out with Earl that night.

"You know, just driving around, maybe go up to town or something like that."

Reluctantly she had said yes. She didn't really approve of Earl, and that feeling had strengthened since she met his father. A typical cowboy. Very polite, some might say handsome too, but with a kind of knowing, over-confident smile she found disconcerting. That cowboy smile carried with it an assumption of his manly power over her. All he had to do was ask. She was only a woman after all.

Archie wasn't like that exactly, but he carried around other assumptions about their relationship. With him they were more money than manly. Even Harold, young as he was, assumed too much, acting as if she actually owed him something. She supposed there was no way to escape from them — goddamn men and their goddamn assumptions.

Archie checked his watch.

"Hey, babe, excuse me for a couple of minutes, will you. I have to call the office."

It was six o'clock. That meant eight o'clock in St. Louis. Enid knew he couldn't be calling his office. Something was up. It made her uneasy. All the more so because her headache had returned and she was nauseous.

Archie was gone about fifteen minutes. When he returned he looked drained, as if something cataclysmic had happened.

"Everything OK?" she asked, anxiously

"Yeah. Great. Ah, fine... How do you feel?"

"Better," she lied. "Thanks."

"Good. That's very good."

He was ill at ease. His gaze strayed unsteadily around the room, eyes not focusing on anything for more than a second or two. He's trying to get himself together to deliver the bad news she told herself. Her stomach fluttered and dull throbbing behind her eyes intensified. Archie put his hands together in front of him as if to pray.

"Listen, babe..."

She closed her eyes. Safeway and the trailer park, here I come.

"Listen, you know when I called from St. Louis? From the airport? I said I had something to talk to you about. Well, it's sort of difficult really. I've been trying to think of how to explain it and uh... Well, I suppose the first thing to say is that I'm selling up, getting out of the business. You see, I've had this very good offer. A big company from out of town. Wants everything. The factory, the outlets. Everything."

He pointed towards the bedroom.

"My lawyer. They just signed the papers. I wanted to wait, to make sure before I said anything. So now I guess you could say I'm a free man."

He looked directly at Enid and gave her an exploratory smile.

"Or, anyway, sort of a free man, if you know what I mean."

Enid realized she had been holding her breath. She let go.

"I suppose I should be happy, you know? No more cutters, no more work rooms, no more unions, no more tightwad bankers, no more *faygeleh* designers, no more *tsouris*. Ha! And you know what else? No more smart-ass button makers! So, I should be a very happy man. Should be, but I'm not. Isn't that funny. I'm just not happy. Why do you think that is, babe?"

Archie sat on the couch, hands dangling between his knees, shoulders slumped.

It's not about me and him at all, Enid said to herself. It's about his goddamned business! His fucking dress business! The sawed-off old bastard!

Too old, too short.

Echos of her father's indelicate judgement. A ghostly curse on their relationship.

Too old, too short.

Archie neither heard the echo nor saw the fierce look on Enid's face. He was looking inside and thinking about Archie.

"I been in the trade for more than forty-five years, man and boy. Since I was a kid working for my old man on the East Side in New York. Forty-five years. Learning it from the bottom up. Started sweeping the floors, pushing racks, making deliveries. Can you imagine? A lifetime. Yeah, sure. I suppose it'll take me some time to get used to the change, that's all."

He sat up straight, rubbed his hands vigorously and then slapped them together a few times like a basketball coach trying to fire up his team.

"Right. I shouldn't worry. You'll be OK, Archie Blatt! OK! Better than OK, you'll be GREAT!"

Then he noticed Enid, and his newfound enthusiasm for Archie Blatt dissolved. His hands collapsed back into his lap.

"What, babe? What is it?"

"Nothing," she said unable to conceal her feelings.

"It's going to be OK, really. What's the matter, aren't you pleased for me? Gee, at least somebody oughta be happy."

"Of course, Archie. Of course, I'm pleased. It's just a shock. Suddenly to tell me like that. Completely out of the blue."

"Like Harold and your father I suppose?"

"Jesus! Haven't we been through all that already? What do they have to do with it anyway?"

"Well, you know, it's like you had to tell me something and now I have to tell you something. That's all I mean. Come on, babe, don't get so mad."

She lit a cigarette, all thoughts of quitting long since abandoned.

"Anyway, that's the first part. Selling the business. The second part is a little more tricky, but I want you to know that it's going to be alright. I've figured it all out. We'll just have to make a few sort of minor adjustments."

His hands had revived and were weaving the minor adjustments in the air in front of him.

"Going to be alright? Figured out? Adjustments? What are you trying to tell me, Archie?"

"Just let me finish, babe. Please. I'll explain everything. Like crystal. Clear just like crystal."

Warily, watching Enid all the time, he began to speak quickly.

"The thing is that we're, that is Sarah and I, are going to move out here. To Palm Springs. Now that I don't have to worry about the business, I figured who needs the cold and the wet back East. Right? The girls are both in college now, thank God, and the doctor says it would be good for Sarah. The dry heat that is. I thought maybe a little place on that new golf course. You know the one called... what is it?... Eldorado. That's it, Eldorado."

Enid was stunned. The brush-off had come from a completely unexpected quarter. Her father and Harold hadn't been important. All the worrying for nothing. She felt cheated. She felt stupid.

Archie didn't wait for her, he rushed on.

"I know. I know. Listen, now, please, babe. I've thought it out. You and I will simply have to be much more discrete about seeing each other. That's all there is to it. I'll still come over, you know, and, but... well, going out in town together to dinner and that kind of thing is going to be sort of difficult with Sarah here. I'm sure you can see that. Of course, we can still play golf at O'Donnell, maybe even at Eldorado. I mean, there's nothing wrong with that, is there? Sarah won't object to me playing a little golf with friends."

Not a brush-off, she thought, more of a re-negotiation. A good business term — re-negotiation. Like with contracts. It meant she wouldn't have to move out. No Safeway. No waitressing. No trailer park. So, why wasn't *she* happy?

"Well?" Archie asked, with a benevolent smile. "Wadda you think?"

"What do I *think*?" she replied unsteadily. "What *do* I think? I don't know, Archie. I need some time to think... And, of course, there's Harold. What about Harold?"

He opened his arms wide and beamed at Enid. Archie was pleased with himself. Happy almost.

"Don't worry, babe, I got something figured out there as well. When the girls were younger I thought they should go away to school. You know, it would have been a lot easier all around. Me working all the time and Sarah not well. But, Sarah, she didn't like the idea, so they never went. However, I did a lot of investigating at the time and found some great places. He likes horses, right? Well, there was a school in Arizona somewhere. Can't remember the name. Very progressive and big on riding, tennis, all that kind of stuff. It would be a real adventure for Harold. He'd love it. And, if you needed help or anything like that, of course..."

"Of course," Enid said distractedly.

Archie had worked out everything. It was so easy. All her problems solved just like that. She had been silly to worry so much, she told herself. Such a very silly woman.

Enid and Harold

The Lifetime I've Wasted, The Love That I've Tasted

The funeral was simple. Harold, Enid, John, Charlene and a man with a shovel to fill in the hole. She couldn't get a rabbi and in the end decided that Abe could go without one. She cried for herself and because she felt so little. Harold cried for himself and because it reminded him of his parents' funeral, at which he hadn't cried. So, despite the odds against it, Abe Cohen had a tearful family send-off. It was what he would have wanted.

"Well," said Big John, putting a consoling arm around Enid's shoulder, "you gotta think that he's better off this way. He's gone to a far, far better place."

"Sure, honey," added Charlene solemnly, "outta this pail of tears."

"I think," interrupted Big John, "that's 'vale', dear. 'Vale of tears.' "

"Oh, yeah, that's right!" Charlene laughed and immediately clapped her hand over her mouth. "I'm sorry, Enid honey. Didn't mean no disrespect or nothing."

Enid didn't notice. She was still stuck with Big John's first remark. How, she asked herself, could anyone's death be better, except perhaps for the living? No more stench of urine. No more having to listen to his stupid self-pity. No more washing his emaciated body. No more inconvenience. Better for her, that was for sure. But, for Abe Cohen? ... Nothing for Abe Cohen. Six feet under in a place he didn't know and didn't like.

She looked out over the desert which lapped at the low cinder-block wall surrounding the cemetery. The white sand stretched off a few miles to the east until it ran up against the Little San Bernadino mountains, dark pink in the late afternoon sun. Behind the mourners was the highway and the rubber-tire hum of passing traffic. A tumbleweed jumped the wall and bounced across the cemetery in the hot wind. Caught against a tombstone, its dry arms scratched and rattled against the hard surface. Enid shivered.

She had found him in the morning. Lying in bed on his back, eyes and mouth fallen open. It wasn't necessary to take his pulse to know he was dead. Rigid, with skin like yellow wax. There was no mistaking the signs. She couldn't remember whether she had said goodnight to him.

She called the doctor and then Harold.

"Does that mean I can I bring my stuff back?" had been his first question.

"Harold!" she said, shocked by his indifference, "your grandfather has just died!"

"I know that," he replied stolidly.

She decided it would be impossible to make him feel what he didn't, what she didn't. It was just that she thought they both should feel something, besides relief.

"Does anyone wanna say any last words?" asked the man with the shovel.

He looked as if he wanted to go.

"No," said Enid, wiping her eyes. "No last words. You can fill it in now if you want."

They turned and walked towards the car as the first shovelfull of dirt thudded on the lid of Abe Cohen's coffin.

* * *

One of Harold's records was blaring out from the small phonograph in the corner of the room. Enid smiled at her nephew, trying her best not to dislike his music. The music was obviously something so very special for Harold.

"How nice, darling."

"Yeah?"

You could say a lot of things about Howlin' Wolf, but he didn't think "nice" was really one of them. Still, Aunt Enid was trying. He had to give her that.

They stood together in the middle of the empty room, paint

brushes held loosely in their hands. Enid wore an old pair of Levis cut off short and a blouse with the tails tied around her waist. Her hair was up and covered with a scarf. She hadn't worn such clothes for years, since she left Lockheed in '49. She had never done any painting. Neither had Harold.

Through the first thin coat of white paint they could see the roses still pumping out their redness as they struggled to hold onto the light.

"One more coat don't you think, Harold darling?"

"Yeah," replied Harold, "I think so. One more coat."

He was pleased that the room was finally being painted. The roses would be buried, but more importantly the fresh paint made it his room. Not Aunt Enid's dressing room. Not the room in which his grandfather died. His room. It reassured him and he needed reassurance after what she had said the previous day.

"But, Harold darling, it's not only a very good school but it will be fun. They have riding, and they take you on camping trips. You'll be with lots of kids your own age. And..."

"I don't wanna go," he insisted, jaw tight set.

"It will be fine. Really it will, darling. You will be home for the summer and for Christmas. At Easter they take the entire school down to Mexico. Doesn't that sound exciting?"

He wouldn't answer. Arms folded he stared at the floor.

"Harold, there is..."

Enid stopped. She sighed, reached over and ruffled Harold's hair. He looked up at her, questioning. She grinned.

"Yeah, I know, darling. I know you don't want to go. And you know something? You don't have to. The hell with it! Right? The hell with it all!"

The decision had been growing since Archie explained the new regime to her the previous Sunday. Then she was so bruised and sick, so preoccupied about her father, so relieved that she and Harold weren't going to be thrown into the street that she had swallowed her anger and her pride. She persuaded herself that she should at least try it, if only as a temporary arrangement. Besides she had Harold's future, not to say his present, to consider.

"You know something, babe? It'll be better than before. Sure. Now I'll be able to see you any time I want. Don't have to wait for an excuse to get away and then fly 2,000 miles. Won't that be great? We can even go up to LA together once in a while."

"That's just wonderful, Archie."

He didn't hear the defeated irony. He was too busy promoting his new life.

He left on the plane for St. Louis the next day. He said it was business. Something to do with the final arrangements of the sale. She was still having her period.

After his departure Enid's doubts and misgivings grew increasingly corrosive. Archie's wife being right there in Palm Springs, having to hide away, an unpalatable secret in a very small town. Archie sneaking over to see her — no, not to see her, to screw her — that was what it was going to be. No more restaurant dinners, evenings at the Chi Chi, going out to see friends. None of those frills. At long distance and three or four times a year it had settled into a perfectly reasonable arrangement. Up close and all the time she wasn't at all sure. It was too near Sylvia's version of her life. But then there was the Cathedral City trailer park, nylon uniforms, cash registers, swollen feet. She had looked again and convinced herself that it really would be good for Harold to go away to school. He would like it when he actually got there. Sitting across from him, watching his face she had realized that it didn't matter if it was good for him or even good for her, she couldn't send him away.

"You ready?" she asked.

He nodded and picked up the can. They dipped their brushes and, to the howling of the Wolf, gruff and loud, explaining in twelve softly-jolting bars why this was his last affair, they began to put on another coat of paint.

This time the roses disappeared almost completely.

The End